"So tell me what you're looking for in a man," Mitch said.

"You must be picky to have remained unmarried in Lover's Valley, where marriage is practically in the air everyone breathes and sung to babies in their cradles."

Crystal's hands went to her hips. "I know what you're hinting at—that I never got over you—and it's simply not true."

"Do you want to know why I never married?" Mitch asked, his grin teasing.

"No." She turned her back as if to leave. Her curiosity was burning, but she'd have stuck a pin in her eye before admitting it.

"I've thought about you a lot," he said softly.

Her heart froze. "You have not," she said weakly.

"I have. How could I forget you?"

She couldn't stand it any longer. "Why didn't you show up that night?" she asked in an anguished whisper. "What was it?"

"I can't tell you," he said. "The story isn't mine to reveal...."

Dear Reader,

Have we got a month of great reading for you! Four very different stories by four talented authors—with, of course, all of the romantic exhilaration you've come to expect from a Harlequin American Romance.

National bestselling author Anne Stuart is back and her fabulous book, *Wild Thing*, will get your heart racing. This is a hero you won't soon forget. This month also continues our HAPPILY WEDDED AFTER promotion with *Special Order Groom*, a delightful reunion story by reader favorite, Tina Leonard.

And let us welcome two new authors to the Harlequin American Romance family. Leanna Wilson, a Harlequin Temptation and Silhouette Romance author, brings us a tender surprise pregnancy book with *Open in Nine Months*. And brand-new author Michele Dunaway makes her sparkling debut with *A Little Office Romance*—get ready to have this bachelor boss hero steal your heart.

Next month we have a whole new look in store for our readers—you'll notice our new covers as well as fantastic promotions such as RETURN TO TYLER and brand-new installments in Muriel Jensen's WHO'S THE DADDY? series. Watch for your favorite authors such as Jule McBride, Judy Christenberry and Cathy Gillen Thacker, all of whom will be back with new books in the coming months.

Wishing you happy reading,

Melissa Jeglinski
Associate Senior Editor
Harlequin American Romance

Special Order Groom

TINA LEONARD

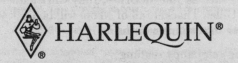

HARLEQUIN®

TORONTO • NEW YORK • LONDON
AMSTERDAM • PARIS • SYDNEY • HAMBURG
STOCKHOLM • ATHENS • TOKYO • MILAN • MADRID
PRAGUE • WARSAW • BUDAPEST • AUCKLAND

Many thanks to all the wonderful people at Harlequin
who have made my career such a success.

ISBN 0-373-16846-2

SPECIAL ORDER GROOM

ABOUT THE AUTHOR

Tina Leonard loves to laugh, which is one of the many reasons she loves writing Harlequin American Romance books. In another lifetime, Tina thought she would be single and an east coast fashion buyer forever. The unexpected happened when Tina met Tim again after many years—she hadn't seen him since they'd attended school together from first through eighth grade. They married, and now Tina keeps a close eye on her school-age children's friends! Lisa and Dean keep their mother busy with soccer, gymnastics and horseback riding. They are proud of their mom's "kissy books" and eagerly help her any way they can. Tina hopes that readers will enjoy the love of family she writes about in her books. A reviewer once wrote, "Leonard has a wonderful sense of the ridiculous," which Tina loved so much she wants it for her epitaph. Right now, however, she's focusing on her wonderful life and writing a lot more romance!

Books by Tina Leonard

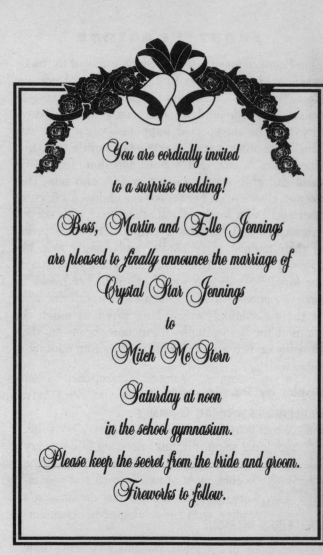

You are cordially invited
to a surprise wedding!

Bess, Martin and Elle Jennings
are pleased to finally announce the marriage of

Crystal Star Jennings

to

Mitch McStern

Saturday at noon
in the school gymnasium.

Please keep the secret from the bride and groom.

Fireworks to follow.

Chapter One

"All I'm saying is that you'd rather have people think you're a lesbian than go out with a man in Lover's Valley, Texas," Bess Taylor declared to her daughter.

"Probably," Crystal sighed as she stuck another pin into the skirt of a bridal gown. "Mother, can you come up with some new lines, please? Just because I haven't dated in a while is no reason anyone would wonder if I've changed my sexual preference."

"It's not normal," Aunt Elle mentioned in her soft voice. "It's not normal that you don't have someone in your life, Crystal."

"Why? Why is it not normal? I have a busy life. I run a bridal salon. I'm busy dressing brides every day of the week. Why is that not normal?" She glared at the contingent of two women and one uncle who were grouped around the dressmaker's dummy, pleading with her to change her bachelorette ways.

Every day in her salon, she saw how tense, how

stressed brides were. If anything, she had less interest than ever in jumping into one of her own beautiful gowns. In fact, she'd pretty much lost interest in men as a subspecies when her high school sweetheart, Mitch McStern, dumped her the night of the prom to go with Kathryn "the Prom Queen" Vincent. If the right man came along, she would regain interest, she was positive. He just hadn't arrived.

She shook her head, perplexed. "Why?" she asked them again. "Why am I not normal?"

"Because you're dressing brides but you don't get married yourself," Uncle Martin stated.

"Oh, and if I were a mortuary owner, I wouldn't be normal unless I died. Then I would be experienced, right?"

Aunt Elle touched her shoulder. "We want you to be happy. You can't go on living other people's dreams forever. We think you should go away for a while, Crystal. Let us run the business for you."

"Go find a man, honey," her mother joined in. "He's out there somewhere."

"I doubt it. And even if he was, I'm sure I wouldn't run into him." She hadn't enjoyed the pain of being left for another woman. Or left at all. She'd learned fast from that one experience. "I'm happy. Why can't you three see that?"

She stared up at her family. They loved her, they really did. Why couldn't they see that she didn't need a man to feel complete?

"I'm getting old, Crystal," her mother began.

"Please don't start playing that harp. You've been playing it since I was twenty-five."

"And I've been more than patient! You're going to be thirty tomorrow! What next? Forty?"

Crystal tried not to smile at her mother's horrified tone. "Look, Mom, if it was that easy, I'd get married just to make you happy. But it's not. Great guys just don't grow on trees, okay?"

"*They're* all happy." Uncle Martin pointed out the window. "See all those couples walking along, enjoying a June summer day in Lover's Valley, the closest thing to God's country?"

Crystal was slowly losing command of her serene posture. "I do. But they're not me! If it was that simple, if I could just reach out the door and grab an eligible male, don't you think I would?" She wouldn't, but she wanted to win the argument and send her relatives home so she could finish the last-minute alterations on a dress for a bride who'd enjoyed marital relations a little too soon and now couldn't be shoehorned into her gown.

"You might not do it, but I would!" Aunt Elle cried, her normally soft voice growing loud with daring. "I'd reach out the door and grab the first man I could if you'd just agree to go out on a date with him, Crystal Star Jennings! I can't bear the thought of you being a wallflower all your life."

"Well, then go ahead," Crystal said through gritted teeth. "But don't blame me if the guy you grab is connected to a furious wife. I'll swear I had nothing to do with it. I have a weapon, and I'll protect myself.'' She brandished the pin cushion, which cuffed her wrist.

"Go ahead," Bess urged. "She said she'd go out with any single male you pulled in. It's just like fishing, sister. Catch us a big one!"

"All right! I will!" Aunt Elle got to her feet. Uncle Martin held the door open and Bess held Elle by the back of her summer dress so she could lean far out into the path of pedestrians—and latched onto the first male sleeve in reach of her fingertips, pulling it with all her might into the bridal salon.

Crystal's jaw dropped when Elle reeled in her catch, a six-foot-two, ebony-haired, bedroom-blue-eyed hunk...of Mitch McStern. "Not you again!" she exclaimed, wishing with all her might Aunt Elle's delicate fingers hadn't been so dastardly.

"Hi, Crystal," Mitch said.

"Turn him loose, Aunt Elle," Crystal snapped.

"You said you'd go—" Bess began.

"I know what I said. I don't have to fall in with a silly prank. A setup." She turned her back, stuffed the closed sign up in the window and refused to look at any of them. "You can all leave now." She heard feet shuffling, but didn't turn around.

Mitch cleared his throat. "They've gone. It's just me, Crystal."

She told her heart not to beat so fast. She begged her blood not to rush through her veins. With all her will, she pleaded with her ears not to hear the wonderful, heartbreaking baritone of the voice she hadn't heard in thirteen years.

It was no use.

He was probably married. Heaven only knew, he probably had crowns in every tooth, maybe even six children and no less than two extra inches on his waistline, but she'd never gotten over him.

Never.

Chapter Two

"At the risk of appearing obvious," Crystal said to Mitch, "the store is closed."

He knew as well as she did that it was only closed to him. "Please don't throw me out on my ear, Crystal."

The years had left little trace of the girl he'd wanted to dance the night away with at the high school prom. This Crystal was taller, probably five-nine in her stockings if she removed the navy pumps she wore. Her hair was pulled into a serviceable bun-thing, with two red Chinese sticks impaled in the back of the thick honey-blond hair. She might have been trying to give an impression of competence, with her summer dress of navy and white print covering her knees, but wisps of hair had defied the torture of the sticks and escaped, framing her sweet heart-shaped face.

She couldn't fool him. Soft, delicate Crystal was hidden beneath that practical, no-nonsense veneer.

"I have nothing to say to you," she said.

Her brittle voice could match ice for hardness.

"Can I ever make it up to you for not showing up that night?"

"No. You cannot." She drew a deep breath. "Mitch, it might have just been a silly dance to you, but I looked forward to it from the moment you asked me. The crush I had on you was immature, possibly, but it was innocent and deep. Never in my wildest dreams did I imagine you would leave me waiting at home, first sitting upstairs waiting eagerly for the doorbell to ring, then peeking surreptitiously out the window, straining to see if you were walking out your front door." She shuddered, her hand tracing over the wedding gown she'd been pinning. "Silly me, I thought you'd had an accident. A flat tire, or worse, a wreck, on the way home from school. But I believed you were coming." She met his gaze now, her hazel eyes full of remembered pain, before she drew herself upright. "Of course, life does goes on. No need to rehash the past. But I'm certain you can see why I'd prefer not to spend an afternoon of auld lang syne."

"There was a reason," he said softly.

"Which I have no interest in hearing, years after you left me high and dry for Kathryn. I heard you looked very handsome when you were crowned king that night, and that she was a very beautiful queen. One can only assume you realized you had a better chance of racking up that win with someone other than me." Opening the door of the salon, she gestured for Mitch to exit. "I wish Aunt Elle hadn't pulled you in the door, because I'd forgotten about you. It's up to me to send you back out.''

There was little he could do. She didn't want him around, and he couldn't blame her. His heart tugged, a cruel, painful sensation. He had actually come here hoping to talk to her. Aunt Elle's magical fingers wresting him inside had seemed like too kind a fate.

He moved outside onto the sidewalk. She stared at him, her cheeks pink spots in her pale face. Her eyes were huge and her full lips trembled. He remembered quite clearly how those lips felt against his, though he'd been so unskilled at kissing he probably hadn't tapped the vein of pleasure kissing Crystal could offer. They'd been young, and those kisses had been earnest and affectionate and sweetly loving.

''Crystal,'' he said haltingly, ''the night before the prom, when we—''

''Don't say it!'' Her voice came out in an agonized gasp. ''Don't you dare mention that night! If I never see you again, my fondest wish will come true!''

And then she closed the door of the bridal shop.

TRAITOR! HE'D BEEN ABOUT to mention the one thing she'd never told anyone, never would tell anyone. Crystal's heart beat wildly, despite the hand she'd thrown against her chest to calm herself. She could only pray he'd never told anyone about the wistful night of discovery they'd spent in a field, far from prying eyes.

She had loved him so much. Maybe it had been the flush and fury of first love, but all her soul had been behind her giving him the gift of her innocence. She'd thought Mitch would be hers forever.

Nothing was forever. That lesson had been learned the hard way, and it was one she wouldn't forget, no matter how handsome the man Mitch had become. He'd branded her, in some mysterious way she'd never understood—and her heart was still his.

The last thing she wanted was for him to discover that unfortunate fact. It was simply too humiliating to have given herself to a man who'd never thought about her again after he'd—

The mortifying words echoed in her mind before she could stop them. *Gotten what he'd wanted.*

She stiffened. That night of secret loving had happened years ago. She wasn't prisoner to such mortifying memories now. Her life was full. She'd moved past what had followed, her utter despair and the quiet sorrow of her family as they'd tried everything they could to heal her broken heart.

She'd gone off to college and received a business degree. Then she'd opened her own store and dedicated herself to making sure that other women's dreams came true, just the way they had always imagined them. She understood the notions of the foolish, lovestruck heart better than anyone.

And if she closed herself up in her tiny red brick cottage at night and sometimes thought about her youthful lover as she sat with her five cats, three dogs, pair of lovebirds and a teacup, well, that was no one's business but hers.

She was happy with her life, and she was going to stay that way.

"EGADS, ELLE, YOU COULDN'T have done that any worse if you'd rigged it," Martin said. The three dejected family members sat in the dining room of the family home.

Elle's dainty shoulders crumpled with apology. "My goodness," she murmured faintly. "Who would have thought *he'd* be standing outside?"

Bess's lips folded. "We are in hot water with Crystal, you can be sure of that. Why, she looked stunned, rooted to the floor, the same way she looked the night he didn't—"

"Sh!" Elle commanded on a moan. "I simply can't bear thinking about that horrible night. Why, my princess in her pretty gown, and that cad not having the decency to...well, I guess it's murky water under the bridge. The brigand."

"It was, until today," Martin said woefully. "Wonder what they said to each other?"

"I doubt Crystal let him say very much at all. As is perfectly appropriate, I suppose." She sounded uncertain. "If I weren't so shocked to see that scamp, I'd have...I'd..."

"You'd what?" Martin said, sitting up to tap his pipe.

"It's curious that he's back in Lover's Valley,"

Elle interrupted, her voice thin and high with hope. "Do you suppose he was outside the store for a reason?"

"Like buying a dress? I shouldn't think he was the shopping type," Bess stated flatly.

"But what if he knew Crystal owned the Lover's Valley Bridal Boutique? How could he not know? His parents would have told him. Any of his high school jock friends would have told him," Elle said excitedly. "Anybody might have mentioned it."

"Even if he'd decided to try to explain for the prom night that didn't happen," Martin cut in, "his words would fall on deaf ears, so we need not speculate on that. Far better for us to concentrate on how we're going to get ourselves out of the doghouse with Crystal."

"You're right." Bess nodded, though a glimmer of hope had been doused in her soul. "As unmotherly as this may sound, on the eve of my daughter's thirtieth birthday, I would almost be willing to forgive Mitch if he…"

Elle's blue eyes were huge behind her silver-rimmed spectacles perching on her delicate face. "If he what?"

Possibly she was abnormal. Certainly she didn't wish her daughter any further pain. Quite the opposite! She wanted her to experience the joy of happily-ever-after.

Unfortunately, she and everybody else in this room knew that Mitch wasn't the man to unlock her daughter from her self-imposed ivory tower.

"Never mind," she said sadly. "At least we've planned something special for Crystal."

"We've never given her a surprise party before. It should be a lively occasion," Elle said. "I expect to see Crystal smiling then. And maybe she'll forgive us for the shock our meddling gave her today!"

Their hopeful smiles faded as they remembered the undisguised panic on Crystal's face when Mitch had landed among them.

"Or maybe not," Bess said.

Chapter Three

Mitch hadn't known what to expect yesterday upon seeing Crystal. As he'd stood on the pavement, trying to gather his wits to go in and offer a long-overdue apology, he'd tried to imagine what she looked like. If she'd changed at all. How she'd come to open a wedding boutique when she'd dreamed of medical school.

He'd attended med school, and become a surgeon in Dallas. Anything that needed removing or suturing, he could fix with skill. Not broken hearts or shattered souls, his or anyone else's. His work was the physical.

Crystal's appeared to be the stuff of dreams.

Yet, she seemed to studiously avoid any pretense of the romantic herself. No one who had a hot date after work dressed like she did. Gone was the giggly girl who'd loved faded blue jeans and glittery fingernail polish.

The Crystal he'd just met was professional. Not about to let her hair down. Refined. He'd once thought her name suited her, because she glowed with an inner warmth that sent prisms of color dancing over the otherwise plain surfaces around her. In her mother's house, there was a crystal chandelier that sunlight had touched in the afternoons as they sat in the parlor talking about nothing more than rainbow prisms and future dreams. Crystal had been warm and colorful, like those prisms.

Now she was beautiful and icy and without color. Crystal without light.

He fully remembered how much fire she'd once possessed. He wanted a chance to warm her again.

But he was not in a position right now to even dream of warming Crystal. He had troubles of his own right now—which was why he was taking a breather here in Lover's Valley.

Mitch swallowed, grabbing at the invitation that sat before him on the table at his parents' home, where he was staying a few nights as he tried to sort out a family dilemma. His parents lived across the street from the home where Crystal had grown up. She no longer lived there, of course, but Martin, Bess and Elle would never give up the family seat. It was a stately two-story white building, with columns out front that spoke of Southern gentility. People in Lover's Valley wondered why two sisters and a brother still held on to a house that was too big for them to keep up and that would bring them a pile of money should they decide to sell. Real estate in this neighborhood had skyrocketed, due to the wonderful architecture and enormous lots.

When his family moved into town his senior year, he'd fallen immediately head over heels for the girl across the street. She was always in motion, having girlfriends over and boys pick her up in their cars.

He'd decided right then and there that location was everything, and he was in a prime position to win Crystal's heart. He had, the same way he helped the football team or the debate team win, using his determination and his charm to win, convince and score.

She'd been so much more than a score. His lips pressed together tightly as he remembered the way moving into her tight body had felt. Heaven and hell all at once. Pain and pleasure in agonizing extremes. The most beautiful thing he'd ever experienced in his life.

To this day he treasured their fumbling, tender joining.

This invitation to Crystal's party tonight, which had his parents' names on it, would not include him. Mitch knew that too well. Bess would think it rude to hold a party in her house without inviting his parents. All the parked cars and noise in front of their houses would strain a relationship everyone was eager to keep as neighborly as possible. Their families had remained cautious friends, mostly because no one knew of the night of passion Crystal and Mitch had shared.

His name was not on the invitation, because no one had expected him to be in Lover's Valley. Even if they had, he would have only been invited because of Bess's good manners. It was a surprise party, and the worst possible surprise he could give Crystal was to show up on her birthday.

Still, he could send a small token of the esteem in which he'd always held her.

BESS, ELLE AND MARTIN could hardly sit still as they waited for Crystal to arrive. After she was safely in their care, Martin would spirit her off on a convenient "errand," which would take up thirty minutes. This would give the guests time to be greeted and then hidden in the decorated great room. When Crystal and Martin returned, wouldn't she have a nice surprise waiting for her?

Tonight, everything was going to go smooth as velvet. "I'm edgy," Bess announced, as if her brother and sister couldn't tell by her pacing.

"I just hope Crystal shows up." Elle fretted, patting her hair as she stared into a sideboard mirror. "I worry about her deciding to work late or some other foolishness."

"Since she may be slightly put out with us from yesterday, perhaps I should call down to the shop," Martin suggested.

"Maybe so." Bess peered out the upstairs window at the street. "Call her, Martin. Make sure she hasn't forgotten that we invited her over for a 'family birthday dinner.'"

They shared a nervous glance.

"I believe I will. No reason to leave anything to

chance, or to Crystal's work ethics.'' Martin went to the rotary phone that sat atop an old rolltop desk in the hallway. He dialed the number swiftly, then listened for a few moments. ''She's not picking up. Maybe she's gone home to feed her pet menagerie before coming over.''

''You don't think they'll bring him, do you?'' Elle murmured from her place at the window. Without realizing it, she'd been staring at the McStern place ever since they'd gone upstairs to keep their vision trained on the street for Crystal's appearance.

''I should think not!'' Bess stated. ''It would be impolite to do that to Crystal on her birthday. Besides, I doubt he would want to come. I'm sure they had very little to say to each other yesterday. And why should he invite himself tonight when he didn't bother to show up for the big night?''

''I don't know.'' Elle sighed, shaking her head. ''It worries me that Crystal may believe we knew Mitch was staying at his folks and told him to pay her a call at the shop.''

Bess straightened, as if a two-by-four had gone up the back of her dress. ''I may be a nosy neighbor, I may be a bit of a well-meaning busybody, but I would never hurt my daughter. Surely she knows that.''

''We were pretty overbearing in her shop,'' Elle reminded her, ''as we primed the pump for tonight so she'd give extra consideration to all the handsome, eligible men we invited.''

''Yes, but we never suspected…you're right,''

Bess said suddenly. "Maybe that's why she's not here. She's angry with us because she thinks we set her up by sending Mitch down there."

"Well, she has every right to be." Martin put the phone down and took a seat on a cushioned chair in the hallway. "Crystal most probably suspects we were matchmaking. Which we were, just not with our neighbor in mind. We had no way of knowing he'd be in town, and even if we had known..."

He trailed off. Bess thought that was a minor dilemma they'd been spared. "Oh, dear, what a quandary!" She paced for a moment before snapping her fingers. "If Mitch shows up tonight, which would be the height of ill manners, we will endeavor to keep them apart. There are enough rooms in this house to achieve that."

Elle nodded. "That way she'll know we weren't trying to run her life. Uh, aren't trying to run her life."

"Exactly," Bess agreed.

The doorbell rang, and the three shot downstairs. Bess couldn't see anyone through the panes of the front door, so she cautiously opened it.

Outside, a small neighborhood boy staggered under the cumbersome girth of an enormous garden bouquet of salmon-and-white garden roses. Bess recognized the child and relieved him of the burden. "How lovely!"

Martin plucked the note from the roses. "It's addressed to Crystal."

Elle chucked the little boy under the chin.

"Thank you, honey. Are you a secret admirer of Crystal's?" she asked, her eyes twinkling.

"No. He is," the child said, pointing across the street at Mitch's home before speeding off.

The threesome gaped at one another.

"I don't think this bodes well. Crystal's definitely going to think we're up to something," Bess warned.

"I'd read the note, but I think that comes under the heading of spying or snooping, something I'm not ready to stoop to," Martin said, replacing the note in the roses.

"Oh, dear," Elle moaned. "Wouldn't he just complicate things for us on Crystal's second big night? The night we're planning to relaunch her into the dating stream?"

"No need to upset her." Bess swept the flowers into the kitchen, putting them in a vase and burying the card among the stems. "We'll tell her about the flowers *after* the party."

They went into the front dining room to survey the hors d'oeuvres they'd labored over. The tablecloth shone white and lacy under the light. Peach candles glowed in tall silver holders. "I wish she'd come on," Bess grumbled. "I want Martin to run her off on the 'errand' before the guests arrive." All the tension of the evening was beginning to build in her muscles and in the back of her neck. She didn't want anything to spoil the surprise for Crystal. *This should be a night of happiness for my daughter.*

"I'll try her house again," Martin said. "And the shop."

"You need not bother. It'll be a few more minutes before she gets here," Elle said suddenly, letting the lace panel of the drape fall back into place. "She just went into Mitch's house."

CRYSTAL HAD TO FORCE herself to move past Mitch into the hallway. Her heart beat quickly, enough to make her feel even more nervous than she already was. He stared at her with curious eyes, and every instinct screamed that she'd made a mistake in coming. "I want to apologize for my behavior yesterday," she said, her tone crisp to cover her discomfort. "Not that I appreciate the joke that was played on me, of course. But I overreacted to something that was, after all, only a joke."

His eyes widened. "I didn't play a joke on you, Crystal. And I certainly understood your reaction. Actually, I was quite stunned to be jerked inside your store."

"It's hard to believe you," she murmured. "My trio of loving family members had just been stating their feelings about my unwed status. And then, presto! Available high school boyfriend appears, like a canned man. Instant relationship. Or at least I suppose they'd hoped it would be."

"I'm not available," he corrected her, "nor would I be a candidate for a canned man, as you put it."

Her lips parted just a fraction, though she caught

herself before her mouth fell completely open. "Not available! I haven't heard anything about you being married." Then she blushed, because she had as much admitted she'd been keeping an ear attuned to his bachelor status.

"Oh, you mean available as in *unmarried!*" he exclaimed, as if he hadn't known all along that was what she'd meant. A twinkle gleamed in his eyes. "Since you're inquiring, actually, I am currently unattached."

"I was *not* inquiring," Crystal said, her feathers totally ruffled. "It makes no difference to me at all. I'm a very happy single woman, and I couldn't care less about any man!"

"Ooh, that sounds angry." He pulled her by the hand into the sitting room. "Care to talk to me about it?"

"No!" Jerking her hand out of his, she glared at him.

He appeared nonplussed. "Oh. I just thought maybe you had some issues with men you'd like to talk about."

"I wouldn't discuss them with you, even if I did have men issues, which I most certainly do not!"

"Well, clearly something's going on, if your family is jerking strange men off the street to go out with you." He sucked his teeth in a "poor Crystal" emphasis as he shook his head. "Think of me as your big brother, ready to counsel you."

If Crystal could have steamed, she would have. "The last person I would ever want to help me with any psychological trauma is you. You are no big brother figure in my life, Mitch McStern!''

''I see it now,'' he murmured.

''See what?'' she demanded, cursing herself for falling for his ploy.

''That fire you used to have. Ah, Crystal, I thought you'd lost your shine for good. All you needed was a little heat, and the radiance is reflecting right back off your transparent heart.''

He pulled her into his arms, giving her a kiss that was guaranteed to melt any remaining ice she might have possessed. Crystal struggled at first, outraged, before slowly allowing herself to give in to the memories. He still kissed the same, wonderfully gentle and deep, taking his time with her. She was special in his arms. He had the power to make her feel that way. If he was heat to her ice, she was liquid water now, flowing smooth and wet.

She gasped when he pulled away from her. His hand swooshed a fast smack to her fanny, and she jumped away from him as if lightning had zapped her. ''Oh!''

''A kiss for good luck, and a spanking to grow on. Happy birthday, Crystal.''

''How *dare* you?'' He stood looking at her smugly, and Crystal wanted to smack him upside the head with a sofa cushion.

The phone rang, startling both of them. She whirled to leave.

''Uh-uh,'' he said, grabbing hold of her wrist.

"No running off in a huff or the previously offered apology is moot."

"I'm not apologizing for being angry now!" Crystal tried to loosen her wrist but she couldn't. His grip was strong, and his grin was huge. He was toying with her!

He reached to answer the phone, and she considered sending a fast kick to his ankle. But he shook his head at her, warning her in case she made that mistake. The way things were going, they'd end up on the floor in a wrestling match, and that would do no good for the little composure she had left.

"Elle? How are you doing? I haven't seen you, well, since yesterday, I guess. I would have liked to spend more time with you and Martin and Bess," he said, catching Crystal's complete attention. "Everything happened so fast. Maybe next time we can visit longer. Why, yes, she *is* here," he practically crooned, enraging Crystal totally. "We were just remembering the good old days."

Wildly, Crystal tugged at her wrist, determined to get away from him. Without seeming to pay her much attention, he drew her against him, holding her tightly against his side.

"Sure. I can do that. You, too, Elle."

He hung up the phone and grinned at her.

"They're expecting me. Let go of me," Crystal commanded.

"I can't. They said they can't meet with you for another thirty minutes, and would I mind keeping you occupied in the meantime. I said I was more than happy to do so.''

''I don't need to be kept occupied!''

''Your aunt Elle said you did. And I'm delighted to do my neighborly duty.'' He ran a finger along the side of her face, brushing back the wisps of hair that now escaped the dangerously loose knot.

Traitorous chills raced through her veins. ''Mitch, let me sit on the sofa. I don't want to be this close to you.''

He let go of her. ''Methinks you protest too much, but that's okay. You always had a hard head. Let's sit down and chat about our schoolmates.''

''I don't want to make idle conversation.'' Her heart was still hammering from their kiss. How could he act so nonchalant about it? No one had ever kissed her the way he did. Sadness overwhelmed her. The truth was, she did want a man—the right man for her! How could she ever find him when he had to compete with what Mitch could do to her with a simple kiss?

''Oh, don't be a spoilsport.'' He patted the leather sofa where he'd taken a seat. ''You're safe with me. Your aunt asked me to keep you company for a few minutes while they finish cooking something. You can stay here without losing your cool.''

Her temper began to rise again. ''I believe you grabbed me, not the other way around.''

''Well, a guy should remember his ex-girl-friend's birthday, or he wasn't much to start with, right? I like to think I have some romantic qualities.''

She ground her teeth, not taking the seat he'd offered. He lounged on the leather sofa, completely unaffected by her stern expression. "Any guy who has two dates to a senior prom most certainly has delusions of romantic grandeur. As for me, that's not what I look for in a man."

He perked up. "So tell me what you are looking for. You must be picky to have remained unmarried in a town like Lover's Valley where marriage is practically in the air everyone breathes, piped through the water systems, and sung to babies in their cradles. And you run a bridal shop, too." He shook his head. "Maybe you got hung up on one man and couldn't find anyone to live up to him."

"Absolutely not!" Her hands went to her hips as she glared at him. "Mitch, I know what you're hinting at, that I never got over you, and it's simply not true. I've dated a lot of men. I am waiting for the right one. There is no good-through date stamped on me, I'll have you know!"

"Lucky for you this is the twenty-first century, or you'd be called a spinster, you know," he said, his tone reasonable. "I've always thought that was such an ugly term. Spinster, maiden aunt, it all speaks to lonely, unloved existences, in my mind."

"Thankfully, your mind is not what counts where I'm concerned," Crystal snapped.

"Don't you want to know why I never married?" Mitch asked, his grin teasing.

"No." She turned her back as if to leave. "I am not going to play this ridiculous game with you. I knew that was what you were leading up to all along." Her curiosity was burning, but she would have stuck one of her straight pins in her eye before she admitted it.

"Okay," he said agreeably. "We won't talk about me. Let's talk about you. Now that you're a successful business owner and an avowed recluse, what's the next goal in your life plan?"

"To live through the next fifteen minutes with you," she said between gritted teeth as she turned to stare at him again. "Why I ever thought I needed to apologize to you is beyond me." Why she still found him attractive was another mystery, too unpleasant to delve into deeply. *Why, why, why?*

And he seemed to know her thoughts as he reclined against the sofa arm, gazing at her. His eyes sparked with mischief and reckless fun, much the same as in more youthful days. But now...now he was so much more handsome. No young boy, but a grown man broad of chest and shoulders, his muscled arms not nearly concealed enough by the clinging white polo shirt. Darn him. Though his eyes were still those of her teenaged Romeo, his face had planed into maturity. A five o'clock shadow surrounded well-formed lips, those lips that had just left her breathless with a kiss every bit as heartstealing as their cherished kisses of the past.

"Now, Crystal, admit you're glad to see me."

"I don't think telling lies is honorable."

He vaulted over the sofa back to stand in front of her. "I'm glad to see you," he said softly. "I've thought about you a lot."

Her heart froze, suspended like a cold rock in her chest. "You have not," she said weakly.

"I have. How could I forget you?"

She couldn't stand it any longer. Common sense told her she didn't want to know, but her foolish heart was already crying to know the answer. "Why didn't you take me to the prom?" she asked on an anguished whisper.

"I wanted to. I was looking forward to it." He reached up, finally snagging the red Chinese sticks and removing them so that her hair fell to her shoulders. Laying the sticks on the sofa table, he pulled her into his arms. "I couldn't," he said, brushing a kiss against her lips. "I just found myself in a position I couldn't extricate myself from," he murmured against her mouth, before tasting deeply of her.

He pulled back and his words brushed her lips. "Crystal, I tried to talk to you a hundred times after the prom, and you ignored me every time. You wouldn't return my calls. Never replied to my notes—which, by the way, I saw torn up in the trash after we cleared out our lockers. You didn't attend our graduation night party, and I knew then that you'd avoid me at any cost.

"And you did, didn't you, Crystal? And today I've just teased you a lot to keep from scaring you off again. I didn't want to lose you then—'' but I can't have you now, he finished silently.

Crystal clung to him as if there were no tomorrow. There were no family members waiting on her, no birthday dinner with just her relatives woefully eyeing the carefully counted candles on her homemade birthday cake. She was seventeen again, and nothing would ever come between her and Mitch. Nothing.

''What was it?'' she asked on a gasp, feeling his thigh part hers and push against the serviceable dress she'd worn to work.

''I can't tell you,'' he said. ''All I can tell you is that I wish it had been you I was with that night.''

Stunned, she stared up into his eyes. He ran a thumb lightly over her lips. ''Why can't you tell me?''

''The reason is confidential. I would be breaking Kathryn's confidence to tell you.''

Splinters of jealousy flew into her heart. ''I was never sure how Kathryn got to be part of our big night. When did the two of you get to be such good friends?''

''She had a problem that she came to me for help with.'' Mitch gazed at her, his expression longing. ''I can say no more than that. You have to trust me, Crystal. I wanted to be with you.''

A long moment passed as she weighed whether she really wanted to ask the question that popped into her mind. Most likely, she didn't want to know. ''Did you kiss her?'' she asked, her face flaming as soon as she said the words.

After a moment, he gave a single nod. Crystal's heart shattered all over again. There was nothing else she would ask, because he'd given her the answer she needed. He'd made love to her the night before; she'd thought their shared first time meant something.

But he'd kissed Kathryn the very next night.

"I have to go! I have to get out of here."

She flew to the front door and outside before he could stop her. Sprinting across the street, she noted that her house was brightly lit, which was unusual. Her family was usually very energy-conscious. But she had to get away from Mitch and their past and the pain, and she couldn't stop to admire how pretty the house looked with all the lights bedecking the evening.

She threw open the door and slammed it behind her, gulping air as she realized she'd left her hair ornaments at Mitch's, so that her usual snug do was a tousled mop. Her lips had been kissed of lipstick and felt larger than normal. She had to get her makeup on and her hair up before her family's sharp eyes noticed—

"Surprise!"

Crystal screamed as it seemed a hundred people leapt out at her from behind sofas and curtains and tables. Her hand flew to her throat and then to her uncustomarily mussed hair.

The added shock was too much for her already skittish blood pressure. Before Crystal could stop herself, she slid to the parquet floor in a faint.

Chapter Four

Crystal thought she was waking from a nightmare when she opened her eyes to see Frank Peters staring down at her. "Are you all right, Crystal?" he asked.

Even in their high school days, Frankie had been a menace. Girls weren't safe in his car. He was too darn handsome for words, and he by golly knew it.

She wanted no part of him. "I'm fine," she whispered. *Now go away, nightmare.*

Lincoln Lark, who'd once held the record for most yards rushed in a season for the Lover's Valley Vikings, tried to help her to her feet. "Let me carry you," he offered. "I'll put you on the sofa."

Lincoln hadn't come by his record by accident. He rushed for yardage the same way he rushed for women. Crystal wanted no part of him, either, having seen him snap the back of homely Penny Parson's bra while she was fishing around in her locker. He'd laughed uproariously at her yelp of surprise and pain. Crystal hadn't thought the "turtle snap'' was very funny. "Go away, Lincoln," she said, as gently as possible, giving him a little push. "I can get up by myself."

"Aw. You're always saying you can do everything by yourself, Crystal Jennings." Barney Fearing was the third head that clouded her vision. "Only woman in Lover's Valley who'd have three strong, handsome men offer to help her, and stubbornly stay lying on her back just to show everybody how independent she is. Come on, you old party pooper. Can't believe you hit the ground at your own surprise party."

She eyed Barney, her gaze narrow. He was always less tolerant of her than the other high school guys, possibly since they'd once gotten into a water-balloon-throwing contest and she'd hit him square in the zipper so that he'd gone around for a couple of hours looking like he'd peed his jeans. Not only that, but the balloon had hit him hard enough to send the color rushing from his face. The girls had cheered her, but Barney had been respectful of her aim after that. He'd begun treating her like a kid sister he had to protect.

He wasn't acting so brotherly now. She frowned at him.

He ogled her legs. "If you don't get up, I'm going to forget I'm a gentleman and look up your dress. When you faint, Crystal, you show a maximum amount of skin."

She gasped, and either he pulled her to her feet or she shot there by furious propulsion.

"Jes' kiddin'," he said with a toothy grin.

But she'd gained her feet only to come face-to-face with Mitch. Crystal stifled a moan, wondering if she'd pass out again.

"Here, Doc," Barney said. "This is the most hardheaded woman in all the valley. Got a cure for that?"

The room became still as night. Crystal flushed cold all over. Not a single soul in the room was unaware that Mitch had dumped her. Fascinated curiosity captured everyone's attention.

He eyed her coolly, assessing, most likely, the mark he'd left on her unruly hair and swollen lips. "Haven't seen one in the *Physician's Desk Reference*," he said maddeningly. "Hardheadedness isn't something that necessarily demands a cure, though. And should the patient want to be cured, that would require a doctor of psychology. It's not my field." He winked at her, playing to the audience.

"What are you doing here?" she demanded, exasperated with his audacity.

He shrugged. "When you fainted, Mom called me over to check you out. Are you all right?"

"I'm fine." She'd been completely fine until he'd stormed back into her life. "I've never fainted before. Never. You needn't have bothered yourself on my account. I'm sure it was just an allergic reaction to *something*."

He grinned at her.

"Come on," Barney said, hauling her into the

great room. "You've got about a hundred old chums here to talk to. You don't have time to have a panic attack. Me and Frank and Lincoln'll take care of you in case you start getting woozy again."

Crystal groaned inside. She felt physically ill. But her mother and Uncle Martin and Aunt Elle were beaming like sunshine, delighted with their surprise party, and she'd be damned if she'd disappoint them. Taking a deep breath, she smiled at all of the guests crowded into the great room and flowing across the hallway into the parlor. "Thank you all so much for coming," she said loudly. "What a wonderful surprise!"

Then she went over and kissed her family, with her three over-eager knights at her side.

Mitch, she noticed when she glanced over her shoulder, merely leaned up against the door she'd fainted against, his grin as irritatingly wide as a canyon.

MITCH HUNG AROUND, even though his medical services were no longer required. Aunt Elle pressed a drink into his hand, and Martin managed to get him into a discussion about the skin on Martin's upper arm that had turned brown in an odd-shaped patch. Mitch recommended a specialist for him to see, and then Bess spirited him into the kitchen so she could thank him for the roses displayed on the table.

"Crystal doesn't know you sent them," Bess confided. "We didn't have a chance to tell her."

"That's all right."

She didn't say anything to that, and Mitch suddenly wondered why he'd been lured into the kitchen, away from the guests. Away from Crystal. "Is there anything I can do to help?" he asked, wondering if she perhaps had a reason for keeping him in here with her.

"Well, you could put some olives on top of those crackers with the spread on them, and arrange a little garnish beside that cheese ball."

He glanced in the direction she indicated. Tiny olive slices sat atop different types of spread, and perfectly placed rows of crackers lay waiting beside a tempting cheese ball. His lips folded. "You've already done that, Bess."

She looked up, her attention clearly elsewhere. "Oh, you're right. How silly of me."

"Can I carry them out to the guests for you?"

"Oh, no, Mitch. You just sit right down here and make yourself comfortable."

He sat but decided Bess had a motive. "Was there something you wanted to talk to me about?"

"Why, no!" She gave a high laugh. "I just haven't seen you in so long I thought I'd allow myself to monopolize your time for a little while. Neighbor's privilege, you know."

Through the serving window, he could see Crystal being squired around the room by Frankie, Lincoln and Barney. She now wore a feisty red dress with a short, knife-pleat skirt that swayed gently just above her knees when she slow-danced to the three-piece band on the patio. After Crystal had sufficiently gained her footing, Elle had spirited her upstairs to give her a ''birthday present,'' which turned out to be the hot red number and matching sparkly heels. She'd pulled her blond hair up into a glamorous fall of curls and applied siren-red lipstick to her sweet, heart-shaped lips. The severely professional Crystal had disappeared with a wave of Elle's nimble fingers. He had to give them credit: Elle and Bess on a manhunt for Crystal was a formidable quest. One of those unsuspecting but eager lunkheads drooling on Crystal would find his finger skewering a wedding ring if he wasn't careful.

He shook his head. ''So this isn't a surprise party as much as open season for Crystal.''

Bess's fingers hesitated over the cucumbers she was paring. ''Whatever do you mean?''

''The knights invited to pay court to your daughter.''

She gave him an innocent look. ''I have no idea of your meaning, Mitch. We merely invited everyone who was still in Lover's Valley who was Crystal's age and our acquaintance.''

None too smoothly, Frankie put his hand at the small of Crystal's back, only to collide with Barney's hand, which was already there. Both men jerked their hands away from Crystal and glared at each other. Lincoln took advantage of this break in bodily possession to claim Crystal for a dance. Mitch grinned at the pained look on Crystal's face, though it was instantly replaced by a polite smile.

He shifted on the chair and snagged a cucumber

from the neat row Bess had sliced. She smacked his hand without rancor and continued cutting.

"You look very nice, Bess." It was the truth, but he could tell his compliment flustered her. She wore an elegant dress of blue silk, long-sleeved and to her knees, perfect for church.

"Don't flatter me, Mitch. It's not *my* big night," she told him, her tone brisk.

"Well, maybe I should go tell the bride—I mean, the belle of the ball—how nice she looks."

"No!" The line of cucumbers she'd been nervously slicing fanned into disorder as her head jerked up. "I mean, don't go just yet."

Grabbing a cracker off the round plate, he popped it into his mouth, trying to figure out what Bess really wanted. After a second, he had it. "I get it. You don't want me around Crystal. Why didn't I see that?"

"Not necessarily, Mitch," Bess said, her tone lacking conviction. "We let you have half an hour with her while the band was unloading and the guests arrived."

"Oh, I see. And now I shouldn't monopolize her because the other guys need a shot at her, right?"

Bess pursed her lips. "Any person who is being honored with a party in his or her honor makes certain every one of the guests has a moment of his or her time," she informed him huffily.

"And technically, I'm not a party guest."

"No, technically you've already had your moment with Crystal this evening," Bess reminded him. "This isn't personal, Mitch, it's simply good etiquette. Besides, I haven't seen you in ages. I didn't even know you were in town until...until we saw you at Crystal's shop."

He tapped the older woman lightly on the hand, which had ceased chopping the cucumbers. "You've chosen bachelors number one, two and three. I'm not part of the equation."

Bess sighed and shoved the vegetables into a bowl. "I'm not matchmaking, Mitch. If I were, I'd make certain any good male with decent financial prospects was within reach of Crystal. I'm keeping you in here with me because you're trouble."

"Why am I trouble?"

She smacked the knife down onto the counter. "I may be old, Mitch McStern, and I may not have a medical degree, but anyone with two eyes in their head could see the fit Crystal was in when she returned from your house. Why, she practically flew in here like demons were after her! And," she said, wagging a finger at him, "don't think I didn't notice that Crystal's lip gloss was on your lips when you came rushing over to attend to her faint."

He rubbed quickly at his lips, but they felt the same as always.

"I thought so," Bess said softly. "Guilty, Mitch, guilty." She took a deep breath. "You understand that you can't play with her heart now, don't you, honey? There's no way I can allow it. If her father was alive, I'd have him speak to you, but as it's just me and you've brought up the subject, I'll have to be blunt. Your senior year romance put Crystal off dating for a long time. She never did let her heart go into anything after that. Now she lives other people's dreams. This time," Bess said, tapping Mitch on the chest, "you stay away. Please. She shouldn't have to lose another thirteen years of herself just because you've blown back into town."

"Bess, it was your—"

"I'm sorry, Mitch." Her large hazel eyes filled with tears. "You say I'm husband-hunting for Crystal. I say, you're right. Is that so wrong, Mitch?" She swallowed, her lips moving convulsively. "She is the child of my heart, my only child. Is it so wrong that I want to see her happily married like her father and I were? Is it wrong to want that for my daughter, my only child, the light of my existence? Did you ever think about her name, Mitch? Crystal Star. Some people might think that was silly. Some might think it was hoity-toity." She exhaled, shaking her head. "In my eyes, she is as beautiful as crystal, as radiant and special as a mystical star." A measure of time passed before she spoke again. "I've been patient with Crystal all these years, knowing her heart was shattered. But a mother sometimes has to provide the nudge. I don't think I'd be doing my duty by my daughter if I didn't act in her best interests. She's thirty years old tonight, Mitch. If I could put it in a box, I'd give my only child lifelong happiness for her birthday—and true love. Can you offer her that?"

They stared at each other for a long time. Bess's gaze didn't falter. Mitch shook his head.

"I'm glad we had this talk," he said.

"So am I." Bess went back to arranging a tray. "I don't need you out there making the other guys suffer by comparison."

Mitch grinned at her. "Give me the knife. I'll practice my surgical skills on those cherry tomatoes."

She sniffed and scooted knife and tomatoes his way. "I've got enough vegetables set back for canning that I can keep you in here chopping all night."

He laughed out loud. "I might as well stick around and see which sheikh Crystal chooses."

"Don't interfere," Bess said, pointing her finger at him again.

"Wouldn't dream of it," he agreed, pointing right back at her, imitating her bantam stance.

Bess sighed, but it was rueful. "The day I laid eyes on you when you first moved here, I knew you were trouble, Mitch McStern. I said, that boy's gonna be a real heartbreaker."

"No, ma'am," he assured her. "I'm a heart-fixer. Says so on my medical degrees."

"We've already had enough excitement this evening with Crystal fainting. You just sit in here, son, before you get my blood pressure up so high I end up busting a valve."

"I'd fix it," he assured her, his eyes twinkling.

"The last thing I'd ever want you doing is messing around in my chest cavity,'' Bess stated. "Just sit right there where I can keep my eyes on you, and maybe the rest of this evening won't end up being a disaster!''

CRYSTAL DUTIFULLY DANCED with Frankie a second time, promising herself that since she'd now given each of the football legends a second dance, she would make herself go over and say hello to Mr. and Mrs. McStern. Mitch's parents talked and laughed with another couple from Lover's Valley as they watched the slow-circling couples move around the floor. Obviously the McSterns were having a good time, so Crystal tried not to feel guilty that she hadn't gone over to them. Mrs. McStern had been concerned enough to call for help when Crystal fainted—and even if she had summoned the man responsible for Crystal's attack of lightheadedness, Crystal owed her thanks. *After this dance I will do it, and just hope Mitch doesn't try to talk to me when I do.*

Of course, he hadn't made much effort so far to get within a foot of her. Maybe dancing with the birthday girl was a pleasure he was willing to forego since he'd already had the pleasure of kissing her spineless. When Crystal had danced with Lincoln, she'd kept her body turned just enough that he couldn't rush for yardage past the scrimmage line of her waist. Hampering Barney from holding her so tightly that everyone would assume an engagement was in the offing was a feat, but she managed it. Now, she had to deal with Frankie.

During all this nearly body-bruising physical maneuvering, somehow her eyes kept seeking out Mitch on the stool in the kitchen, keeping her mother company. She didn't mean for her gaze to wander to him, but when she began to develop a headache from her body being moved one way while her eyes went another, she forced herself to quit surreptitiously glancing his way. Even though she told herself he didn't notice her furtive assessment of him, her feelings were somehow hurt that he paid more attention to wheedling snacks out of her mother than to her. The way he'd kissed her had put zing into her heartbeat for the night. *I'm still not over him,* Crystal realized sadly.

It depressed her, all the more so because he never looked her way. Frankie slid his hand too near the curve of the wow!-red skirt, which fell in a pleat over her posterior so nicely. A seamstress like Crystal couldn't fail to appreciate the craftsmanship of the dress, but she absentmindedly ground the red high heel Aunt Elle had insisted she wear onto his toe. He gasped in pain but she merely smiled, her expression innocent.

"Good thing there's a doc in the house," Frankie wheezed tightly.

Her smile evaporated. "You won't need one if you stop trying to get into the end zone, Frankie."

"Dang, Crystal, how can I help it when you're just about the only unmarried woman in Lover's

Valley who doesn't have horse teeth or a backside broad as a barn?''

"That's not nice," she reprimanded him. "For one thing, it's a prejudicial view, and for another, all those women are high school acquaintances of ours and very sweet."

"I know," he grumbled. "But I don't want to marry a gal who has a great personality. I want to marry a gal that looks like a firecracker in a red dress!"

She eyed him narrowly. If she looked like such a pyrotechnic explosive, why wasn't Mitch blown away? "I think you should reconsider your play options."

He looked at her earnestly. "Truly, Crystal, you're the only woman in Lover's Valley who is single of her own hardheaded choosing. And ain't you ever heard heartbreak is attractive on a woman? Makes a guy just wanna cuddle her and hold her tight," he said, crushing her to him, "and protect her from all the mean old tackles in life!"

She ground her teeth to hold back her reply while she counted slowly to ten, mentally composing herself. The gentler-version reply never formed in her mind as the room suddenly went silent except for the soft orchestral strains from the band.

Kathryn "the Prom Queen" Vincent walked into the great room. She was just as petite as ever, her smile still cheesily bright, ever the cheerleader. But the size of her stomach wasn't hidden by the elegant black dress she wore.

She was heavily pregnant, and she was alone.

Chapter Five

Crystal swallowed as Kathryn's eyes met hers. *Why did my family invite her?* was the first thought that shot through her mind.

Her second thought was that Kathryn looked very uncomfortable, either from her pregnancy or from being the center of attention. It didn't matter. She'd made an effort to dress up and come to Crystal's party, even bringing a brightly colored gift, and Crystal knew good manners like she knew sequins on a bridal gown.

"Kathryn," she said, walking over to the woman she'd once called her best friend. "How lovely of you to come."

"Thank you." Kathryn's voice wavered a little. "Tom couldn't make it. I...I hope it's all right that I came alone."

Kathryn's brown eyes seemed to speak of loneliness. Crystal remembered that her husband, Tom Trent, traveled a lot, the only one of the football buddies who'd ever managed to get past his small-town roots in some fashion.

"Of course it's fine. I'm glad you could be here." She took the present Kathryn offered her, admiring the silver-and-purple wrapping. "Thank you so much."

"It's just something small, a...a small thing to put in your house. I heard you liked animals," Kathryn said nervously, staring up at Crystal.

"Do I ever. Come get a drink. We have Perrier water and a few other things."

"Thank you."

Crystal walked her over to the bar. Her mind flew with a thousand questions, none of which seemed like a safe topic to introduce. Kathryn seemed more ill at ease than ever, and it dawned on Crystal that she couldn't leave the watermelon-shaped ex-cheerleader alone at the drink bar with no one to talk to. And no one seemed in a big hurry to rush over and greet the prom queen.

Crystal frowned as she fixed a Perrier. "How have you been?"

"Oh, fine," Kathryn said airily.

Too defensively flip to be candid. Crystal stared at Kathryn. Long seconds passed. Why wasn't anyone coming over to welcome one of the most popular girls in their class?

Suddenly, Mitch appeared at their side. "Hello, Kathryn," he said warmly.

"Hi, Mitch." The cheerleader's smile was relieved.

"Care to dance?" he asked.

"And keep a brave front?"

"The only other option is to fold in the face of scrutiny." He grinned at her, his expression daring.

After a moment, she nodded. "All right. Ever my knight whether in jeans or a tux."

"Excuse us, Crystal," he said, "Kathryn and I are going to enjoy a dance for old times' sake."

Crystal forced her jaw not to drop, but it was like holding up a concrete bridge. Once again he'd referred to that ill-fated night—so casually! Never mind that he'd gone off to dance with the woman for whom he'd dumped her, a move guaranteed to thrill the spectators. She felt exposed and ridiculed.

Barney Fearing pulled her out onto the floor. "Come on, Miss Red-Hot. Let's not stand there like you just turned to stone."

"Oh, hush, Barney!"

He chuckled. "Not that I expected you to thank me for being such a gallant and pulling you out of a pickle, but you could act like you're enjoying yourself, Crystal. It's bad for my reputation as a ladies' man to have you treat me as if I smell like boiled cabbage."

"I'm sorry." She focused on Barney, making herself take a deep breath so her heart would stop racing. "You're a true gentleman to save me from myself."

"I know," he said with a big smile. "Now, why don't you quit eyeballin' over thataway and affix your purty eyes to my handsome face? That way nobody'll know your heart's bleeding red as that sexy dress."

Some irritation poured into her spine, a little at a time. "Affix my purty eyes to your handsome face?"

"That's right. Is there anything in this room you'd rather be gazing upon?" His grin was wide and gleeful.

Crystal smiled ruefully. "No."

"I didn't think so. Mama always said I was a sight for sore eyes. And I reckon yours are sore as anybody's tonight."

She shook her head. "Barney, you're different from the other men, I'll have to give you that."

"I know. Quality shows."

Crystal laughed. "So...how come you haven't settled down?"

He winked at her. "Because I couldn't go out with my buddies anymore if I did."

"I'm not sure I believe that."

"Sometimes me and Frankie stay over at Linc's until one o'clock in the morning," he assured her.

"But if you had a wife, you wouldn't have to do that."

"Fine lecture coming from the most eligible woman in the Valley."

"I'm not... Eligible isn't how I describe myself."

"How do you?"

"I don't know," she murmured. "Happy?"

"Alone?"

"Well, yes. I have my five cats, three dogs, et cetera, and my bridal salon. I never feel alone," she said, vaguely wondering if she was telling herself or Barney the truth.

"Maybe you and I should get married, since we both think marriage is too much trouble," he suggested.

"Maybe so." She laughed, not taking him seriously. "I don't cook."

"I don't vacuum."

"It would make my mother deliriously happy."

"I'd have to beat the hell out of Mitch every time he came around," Barney continued.

She stared at him, her eyes stretched wide and her smile frozen.

"Jes' kiddin'," he said. "But in the three minutes you've had your eyes affixed to my handsome countenance, I estimate Mitch's looked at your legs once every five seconds."

"My legs?" she whispered.

"And all the rest of ya." Barney waltzed her so that she couldn't glance at Mitch no matter how badly she wanted to. "You two ever gonna get together?"

She frowned at him. "What are you talking about?"

"Jes' seems that you've got some unfinished business, which makes it hard for the rest of us bachelors."

"You just said you preferred being single."

"I know. And you just said you liked being single, so how come you're not insisting you don't want to get together with him?"

He had the slyest grin lighting his face. Crystal sighed. "Barney, you never have given me the respect the other guys did. I think you're still smarting from my good aim."

"You got lucky with that water balloon," he told her. "I was in P.E. class with you, so I know you couldn't hit the basket when you stood right under the net. But it's not that I don't respect you, Crystal. I probably just see myself in you. Kinda lonely, and kinda not sure what to do about it."

She hesitated in his arms, surprised.

He kissed her smack on the lips.

"But at least *I've* got good aim," he said with relish.

AFTER THAT, CRYSTAL AVOIDED the football trio, Mitch and Kathryn as they all stood around talking. She circulated among the other guests, and spoke with the McSterns. After a while, she cut her birthday cake and opened the gag birthday gifts, most of which had to do with her single status. Kathryn's gift was a painted dog bowl that was darling, a fact Crystal reluctantly admitted to herself. She was even more astonished to turn it over and see Kathryn's name on the back. "You painted this yourself?"

"Yes. I did. The invitation said to bring a gag gift, so I hope you don't mind I brought something for your pets."

"I didn't know you were such an artist!"

Kathryn's gaze bounced to Mitch and then back

to Crystal. "I've had a lot of time to myself for the past couple of years. I decided to take up pottery. Fortunately, I'm having a little success with it."

"Wait a minute," Crystal said. "I've got a black teapot and cup at home that reminds me of this. It's rimmed in white and has pink-and-red roses scrolling across the bowl."

Kathryn blushed. "That sounds like my design."

"I had no idea," Crystal murmured, studying the oval shape of the dog bowl. Dogs and dog bones chased across the front in a cheery pattern, and at the bottom of the inside a red beribboned bow was painted. "Thank you, Kathryn. It's almost too pretty to use. But I will."

For some reason, the gift made Crystal a little sad. She finished opening gag gifts, and then, miraculously, the evening drew to a close. With relief, Crystal showed guests to the door. She thanked each one for coming. The band packed up their instruments and departed.

Her family's bright eyes watched her as she closed the door for the final time.

"That was very sweet," she told them. "Thank you."

"Did you have fun?" Bess asked.

"I actually did." Crystal hugged them all. "I'm glad it was a surprise party, because if I'd known I'd be facing that, I would have been nervous for a week. I think your birthday present gave me some extra courage, Aunt Elle." She flipped her skirt to show the perfect pleats. "And the shoes, Mom. And of course the lovely necklace, Uncle Martin."

"There're flowers in the kitchen from Mitch we didn't give you yet," Bess admitted.

She halted, her emotions back on the skids. "Flowers?"

"We're so sorry!" Aunt Elle cried, clasping her hands. "We didn't want you...you know. Upset!"

"So we didn't tell you about them. We were afraid it would ruin your evening," Bess told her.

Crystal went into the kitchen, her heart fluttering as she saw the lovely roses. "Oh, my," she murmured.

"Here's the card," Martin prompted.

"Thank you." She opened it, her pulse beating with excitement.

Happy Birthday to a beautiful lady. Mitch.

She stuffed the card back into the envelope.

"Aren't you going to tell us what it says?" Martin asked hopefully.

"No. It's just typical Mitch. Nothing of substance." Crystal headed for the front door, carrying gifts to load into her car. When she was done, she came back inside and hugged each of them again. "I truly had a wonderful time," she said to her family. "For once in my life, I felt like a real Cinderella."

She blew them a kiss and breezed out the door, her twinkly red heels catching shine from the porch lights.

Bess looked after her daughter wistfully. "May

the clock never strike midnight for you when you finally meet your handsome prince," she whispered.

THE FLOWERS, BESS NOTED immediately, somehow were left in the kitchen. "I don't know that Crystal left them on purpose, but I somehow suspect she did."

"It's possible. Although I was very proud of the way she comported herself, both with Mitch and when Kathryn showed up alone," Elle commented as she began hand-washing china plates.

"Couldn't not invite her," Bess said defensively. "She is married to Tom, and they're both members of Crystal's class. Tom would have heard about the party from Barney, Frankie and Lincoln."

"Goof, Goober and Goobus," Martin stated decisively, reaching for a cup towel to dry the dishes. "Do you really think those leftovers could catch Crystal?"

"No." Bess shook her head. "But they sure did slobber all over her tonight, didn't they?"

"We didn't have to try too hard to keep Mitch away from Crystal, although his eyes might have well been glued to her." Elle examined a crystal flute for lipstick. "Did you intentionally monopolize him, sister dear?"

"I most certainly did. I told him under no circumstances was he to encroach upon Crystal's relaunch into society. It's not fair that just when I decide to help her help herself, he shows up again!"

"Oh, my," Elle breathed. "And he still sat in here with you most of the night. Clearly not cowed by the dragon."

"Oh, hush." Bess waved a silver fork. "He was the perfect gentleman to dance with Kathryn after everyone treated her like she had sand fleas."

"I feel sorry for Kathryn. I think Crystal did, too," Martin said.

"Somehow disaster was averted, and I am thanking my lucky stars it was. When Crystal fainted, I thought the whole evening was going up in smoke." Bess frowned. "You know why she fainted, don't you?"

Martin and Elle swiveled to stare at her.

"Because Mitch had been kissing her."

"Oh, my." Elle perked up. "Did he tell you that?"

"He didn't have to. I could tell by the way she stayed away from him as if he were dog poo. And then when I asked him, he all but admitted it. So I had to tell him to leave her alone. If her father were here, I'm sure he'd do the same." After a moment of self-righteous silence, Bess paused to look up. "He would, wouldn't he?"

The threesome was very still.

"I hope I did the right thing," she murmured. "We did agree that keeping them apart was the proper route."

"Yes, we did." Martin nodded.

"We certainly thought we were acting in her best interest," Elle agreed.

They were quiet again for a moment.

"You know, I've got a sudden hankering for a drive," Bess said. "I need some fresh air."

Martin snapped his fingers. "I forgot to give Crystal her gag gift, didn't I? We could just run it over to her house while we're out for our drive."

Elle raised her eyebrows. "You didn't buy her a gag gift."

His shoulders slumped. "No, I didn't."

"Never mind," Bess said, suddenly energized. "We'll just run these pretty posies of Mitch's by her house. The more I think about it," she said, lifting the salmon-and-white garden roses from the vase, "I'm positive she didn't mean to leave without his gift!"

"MITCH!" CRYSTAL EXCLAIMED after getting out of her car. "What are you doing here?"

He stood on her porch, holding a bottle of something that looked suspiciously like champagne. "Waiting for you, princess."

"Oh, please. That line won't get you in the door." She walked up to him, eyeing the bottle with unease. "What do you want?"

"To talk to you." He held up the champagne to ward off her protests. "Talk only."

"We don't require champagne to talk." She'd had a glass of champagne at her party. Somehow it didn't seem wise to combine more bubbly with heartbreak, no matter how much her every sense called out to give in and enjoy Mitch's very exciting kisses.

"You're right." He smiled, and her resistance registered a devastating crack. "But Crystal, I would really like the chance to speak to you."

She had to step closer to the front door so that she could mentally distance herself from temptation. "I...I have to work tomorrow. And I've celebrated enough, thank you."

"To be honest, I wasn't thinking about your birthday as much as I'm trying to bribe you."

"Bribe me?"

"Unfortunately, yes." He sighed. "I won't deny I enjoyed kissing you tonight, Crystal. But when I went over to your folks' house, your mother gave me a stern lecture about staying away from you. I realized she was right."

Crystal was totally amazed. "I would have thought my mother would push you into my life."

He shook his head. "Quite the opposite. She made me realize how inconsiderate I was to...force my attention on you. I shouldn't have kissed you. I'm sorry."

With a jolt of astonishment, Crystal knew she didn't want Mitch to regret kissing her. In fact, just seeing him on her porch had given her a delicious sense of shivery pleasure. Not that she would allow herself to fall for him again, but the thought that he might still feel something from the past the same way she did was tantalizing. "So, if you're not here to ravish me into a champagne haze, why are you here?''

''Do you mind if I come in? It's something I'd rather discuss somewhere other than your porch.''

No way was she falling for this. Once he was inside her house, she might never get him out. He was still inside her heart, refusing to leave. ''How about if I meet you later this week at the coffee shop?''

For once the smile left his face. ''Crystal, look. I promised your mother I wouldn't pursue you. I won't. I would like to share your birthday with you, I won't deny that. But I really need a favor from you.''

This from the man who'd dashed over to make certain she was only faint and not suffering a medical trauma. She sighed. ''Can we agree on fifteen minutes, then? I really have to get up early in the morning.''

Mitch nodded, handing her the champagne. ''I'll set my watch. It's got an alarm guaranteed to bring police running if I'm not gone.''

Rolling her eyes, Crystal unlocked the door. Three large bodies whistled through the opening, furry heads with enthusiastic tongues licking both her and Mitch, tails whipping their legs.

''No wonder you don't want a man,'' he observed. ''You have your own 'honey I'm home' greeting squad.''

''Sit, Thor.'' She pushed down a giant Great Dane that looked more horse than dog. ''Sit, Igor.

No, Nip. No nibbling on Mitch's trouser leg.'' The rest of the roll call was averted as she shooed the canine crew toward the back door.

"Why so many dogs?" he asked.

"Don't you like dogs?"

"Perhaps in lesser quantities."

"Good. I also have five cats and a few other selections from the pound." She flashed him a smile. "See how ill-suited we are? So, my mother can relax."

"Well—"

"And you can relax now. I'll open your champagne for you."

He let her have the bottle as he glanced down at his trousers. "I suppose I'm fortunate I'm only covered with dog hair. I could have lost a limb."

"Oh, no. They're very civilized."

"All packs have their codes of honor, I guess, although I'm not certain I observed one with Barney, Frankie and Lincoln tonight."

She wasn't going to comment on his remark, even if she let herself wonder for a split second if he was somehow jealous. He walked into the kitchen as she readied the bottle. Just as she was about to remove the cork, he put warm hands over hers, helping lift it from the bottle.

A satisfying pop erupted, and a small puff of smoke rose from the opening. He removed his hands from hers, and shakily, Crystal filled a glass. "Cheers," she said, handing it to him.

"None for you?"

"I don't drink this late."

"Come on, Crystal," he said softly. "Let me toast you on your birthday."

Reluctantly, she filled another glass. He held up his. "Happy birthday to a woman who deserves all the happiness she can find."

She raised her eyebrows. "That's sweet, Mitch. Thank you."

They clinked glasses. Crystal barely sipped hers, but she watched Mitch over the rim. He never took his gaze from hers.

She felt magic try to stir her soul. She sternly commanded it to go away, putting her glass down on the counter as she broke eye contact.

"Kathryn said she was glad she came to the party. She said she had wanted to talk to you for a long time and just couldn't make herself."

Spears of panic went through Crystal's soul. "It's in the past. Besides, she seemed lonely."

"She is. Her husband is divorcing her."

"She's pregnant!" Crystal exclaimed.

Mitch shrugged. "He found someone else."

Crystal walked out into the living room and sank into a chair. "That's what she meant by keeping a brave front?"

"Yeah. No one in the Valley knows yet, but most people are uncomfortable around her because they do know Tom was seeing someone else. They don't know what to say."

"It's a very radical change to go from being the most popular girl to..." Crystal's voice trailed off.

An object of pity, and gossip. "Oh, my. I had no idea."

"Well, your business is weddings and happy-ever-afters, not divorce. She confides in me because she doesn't have many friends here anymore."

"She always smiles so much."

"Sometimes people smile the most when they're in pain. Covers up the misery they don't want anyone to see."

Crystal could identify with that theory. She'd spent the whole evening smiling, not about to let anyone pity her. "So. About the favor you wanted to discuss? I think we have eight minutes left on your watch."

The smile filtered slowly from his eyes. He took a deep breath. "You're really the only person who can help me with this."

Her heart started a slow, heavy pounding at the sudden seriousness in his expression. "What is it?"

"You know I have two sisters, Janet and Genie."

She nodded.

"They're both getting married."

"Oh. Congratulations." She lifted her glass but he shook his head.

"Not quite. My youngest sister is marrying someone my parents object to. As do I, actually."

"Oh, my." She lowered her glass to the table. "I'm sorry. But I don't see how I can help you."

"You run a bridal salon."

"Yes, but—"

He edged forward on the seat. "I could suggest she come to your shop."

"You want me to talk to her!"

"Crystal, it occurred to me tonight that you are the perfect person. You're an older, unattached woman who clearly doesn't see the need for a man in her life—"

"Don't make it sound so stale! Ugh! What was that word you used earlier? *Spinster?*"

"Well, perhaps I spoke too soon. You're happy. You're successful. You're independent, smart, and have wisely waited to meet the right man."

Crystal found herself increasingly irritated by Mitch's thought process. The last thing she wanted was for him to admire her for her "spinsterhood"! "Maybe she's in love with him. Perhaps they are right for each other."

"This will be his fourth marriage. He's forty-seven. Genie is twenty-two."

She found herself empathizing with Mitch even though she didn't want to. Stiffly, she said, "I don't think Genie would listen to me, and even if she would, I couldn't advise her against marriage if it's what she wants."

"Crystal, my parents are heartbroken," he said quietly. "Imagine how much your family wants you to find the right person. If your mother has to cart in a truckload of old acquaintances to revive your dating life, she'll do that, and she'll even warn off anyone she no longer considers suitable. Such as myself."

"I'm sure it wasn't quite that way."

"It was just that way. But I understood. After all, I'm asking the same thing of you. Just a little role modeling is all you'd have to do."

It wasn't the same thing as having to do something with Mitch. She wouldn't have to spend time with him. One short conversation with his sister was all he was asking. Even though she felt pretty certain there was nothing she could do where Genie was concerned, neither could it hurt to talk to Genie. Right?

"I'd take you out to dinner," he offered. "By way of thanks."

"That won't be necessary, Mitch." Crystal stood. "If Genie wants to come by the shop, I'll be happy to talk to her. If she's amenable. But I promise no results."

He stood, too. "Guess I have to leave now?"

"Yes. I think it's best."

Her mind was racing. She wanted Mitch to stay longer, but to allow it would be to risk letting her guard down.

"Do you think you'll ever forgive me for what happened?" he asked huskily.

"I have." She met his gaze evenly. "I think you're a great guy. I just sense danger when you're around."

"Danger?"

"Yes. There are still some feelings pretty close to the surface, I'll admit. And honestly, I don't like the feeling."

"Still want to forget me?" Suddenly, the devil-may-care smile was back.

"With all my heart."

"Hmm. I think you need your heart examined."

Her hand flew to her chest protectively. "Don't you dare!"

He laughed outright. "Only with your permission. But I promise you'd enjoy it."

"I doubt it." More relaxed now that they were on the teasing terms that she could hide behind, Crystal let herself move past him to open the door. "I'm a very cautious woman. I don't do dangerous things."

He snapped his fingers as if he'd suddenly had a monumental idea. "A firmly rooted woman such as yourself sure would be good for my career. We should get married, Crystal."

She laughed out loud at the ludicrous comment. "Why do you need a woman like that?"

"People want a model of responsibility opening up their chests. Surgery is a scary thing. They want a doctor with a pretty, devoted wife, and shiny-bright children. Stability. A portrait of marital bliss hanging in the office foyer. Instant respectability."

"I hear your patient list is longer than a mile. You do just fine without a wife. Anyway, I'll have to restrain myself to only one favor. I'll talk to your sister, and pass on the proposal."

"Are you sure? Once you've experienced your own wedding, you might have a better view of the process."

"I'm enjoying the view from my shop. Thanks, though."

He went onto the porch. "Can't blame a guy for trying."

"That's basically what Barney said tonight. And Linc. And Frankie."

Mitch scowled. "Well, don't listen to *them*."

"I'm not listening to any of you." But his scowl made her smile.

A car pulled up next to Crystal's and Mitch's.

"Mother!" Crystal exclaimed.

"Uh-oh. She's not going to be happy to see me here."

"Wonder what she's doing?" Crystal hurried toward the car.

"Trying to keep us apart, I think," Mitch muttered.

All three of her relatives were in the car, but only her mother got out, emerging from the passenger side. "We brought you your flowers," Bess said to Crystal. "Although I see we could have saved ourselves a trip and sent them with Mitch." Her tone was accusing, a cross between annoyance and gotcha!

"Come on, sister," Elle called from the back seat. "We've run our errand. We shouldn't linger."

They got back in the car and Uncle Martin drove off.

Crystal sniffed the flowers. "Lucky for you Mother doesn't know you also gave me champagne for my birthday. I think she's suspicious of you."

She smiled at him. "Flowers *and* bubbly. And to think that once upon a time all I dreamed of was a wrist corsage."

His lips twisted, as if he wasn't sure if she was teasing him or not. "It's the least I could do." He glanced after the departed car, his expression chagrined. "Think they'll believe I was merely paying a house call on my patient?"

"No. But I won't mention the situation with your sister."

"They'll think I've gone back on my promise not to romance you."

"Did my mother really say that?"

He grinned. "She seemed to think I made the other guys look bad by comparison. I was flattered."

"Won't she be surprised when I choose Barney then?" Crystal asked teasingly.

Horror wiped the grin right off Mitch's face. "You wouldn't, would you?"

"He did say he'd cuddle me and protect me from the bad boogeys in life."

Mitch snorted. "You're too independent to be treated like a doll."

Crystal found herself bristling at his know-it-all attitude. She didn't want him to know her so well after all this time. And yet, they had been in love. It was a fact that had bruised her for years.

But she was over him. She would make sure she was. "*Good night,* Mitch."

"Good night, Crystal." He looked so disappointed as he walked to his car that she momentarily felt wistful. A good night kiss on her birthday would be the perfect ending...but she reminded herself of the danger of falling under Mitch's spell again. She could not count on him. There was no guarantee. He was just as charming and courteous as ever—and that was the problem.

She would fall much harder than he would.

Thirteen years without him reminded her forcibly how foolish she would be to get even remotely close to a fire she couldn't handle. He was handsome. He was wealthy. He was kind. He could have any woman he wanted.

He had not cared enough for her before. The chances of him being the type of man who'd let her down would be too great.

Someone like Barney Fearing—devoted, not so high on the Richter scale of sexy, and not quite so sure of himself—would be a far better choice for a woman who didn't want to end up with a broken heart again.

She went back into the house and let the pack in. They surrounded her with joyful abandon. "I'm not interested in any human male," she told them. "You guys have a reputation for loyalty and bending a listening ear at all the right times and being great company. I'm sticking with you!"

Three tails thumped gleefully.

"Whoever said you were *man's* best friend had it all wrong," she muttered as she walked back to her bedroom. They vaulted into her bed, assuming their usual lounging positions. The five cats headed to the top of the dresser and bookshelves.

Crystal brushed her teeth, took off her makeup and put on a T-shirt. She came out of the bathroom and eyed the canines taking up most of her bed. "Definitely no room for one more body here," she said, sliding under the covers in the last available space. A doggy moat shifted around her feet. She sighed with relief. "Clearly there's no breaching this fortress. I'm safe!"

"THE BOUNDER!" Uncle Martin exclaimed.

"Scalawag!" Aunt Elle agreed.

"Rogue. I should have known better than to think he was hearing a word I said to him." Bess was completely annoyed by Mitch's presence at Crystal's house. "I meant to reintroduce Crystal into society, not reintroduce Mitch into her life. This is not going well."

They sat in the kitchen, drinking tea. Elle laughed softly. "We can comfort ourselves that he was outside the house. She's keeping him at arm's length."

"Where he belongs," Bess muttered. "I'd be happier if he'd go back to his practice."

She got up and stalked the kitchen, pacing the length of the black-and-white checkerboard tiling.

"There's nothing we can do about it," Martin said practically, tapping his pipe on a bowl. "It's up to her to say no."

"Crystal's very good at that. I heard her say it

all night long to Barney, and Linc, and Frankie,'' Elle pointed out.

"Those muttonheads. Brawling over her as if she were a football.'' Bess sniffed. "No wonder Crystal stays single in this town. I vote we return to our original plan of getting her out of Lover's Valley for a while. Maybe send her to Paris on a buying spree. Surely she'd meet an intelligent—''

"Sister.'' Elle cast a wary eye at her older sibling. "She has to tell Mitch no. This time, we stay out of it.''

Bess trembled, her mouth puckering in tiny lines. "I'm having an attack of conscience.''

She sat down and the threesome stared at one another. "Do you ever think that maybe I should tell her the truth?'' she asked, her voice an agonized whisper.

Martin and Elle blinked at her.

"A mother's conscience handles a lot over the years,'' she told them. "It whispers endlessly to her over time. One tries to do the very best for her daughter, her only star, the light of her life. I thought…oh, dear,'' she said, tears filling her eyes. "I don't know if I can go any longer without telling Crystal that I was the reason Mitch didn't show up for prom night!''

Chapter Six

"The trouble with Mitch," Genie confided, "is that he's just so old-fashioned! Beyond old-fashioned. Major fuddy-duddy, if you want to know the truth. No matter how much I love him, we just don't see eye-to-eye on much of anything."

Crystal eyed the "blushing bride." Mitch's little sister was dressed in blue-jeans cutoffs that bared more cheek than necessary, and a silver foil spaghetti-strap shirt. She had a rose tattoo just under her collarbone, and a gold stud earring through her bottom lip. Hair the color of ripe raspberries flew in a mousse-thick shock away from her face and ended at her chin.

"I can see that the two of you might occasionally have a difference in opinion," Crystal said carefully.

"But it's cool of him to ask you to help me, Crystal. He's the only one who seems to understand that I *am* going to marry my fiancé. My parents won't even acknowledge my engagement ring."

She held up a hand, showing a silver braid on her finger.

"It's pretty." Crystal shied away from family comments and decided to stick to the issue of dress, a topic that, for once, she felt unprepared for. She knew how to make women into gorgeous, fairy-tale brides. Whether she had anything in her shop that would fit Genie's idea of happily-ever-after fashion she wasn't certain. "Let's find a dress to go with your lovely ring."

"Okay."

Genie hopped up to follow Crystal, and Crystal noticed a silver toe ring on Genie's bare foot that matched the ring on her finger. Slight envy curled through Crystal, surprising her. She wasn't exactly a toe-ring kind of girl. Maybe it was the spontaneous, free attitude the ring represented. "Do you have an idea of what you want?"

"Not really." Genie looked like a sorbet-haired elf amid all the frothy long wedding gowns and veils. "Maybe you could show me something *you* would like."

"Something I..." Crystal's voice trailed off. She'd never stood in her store and imagined a gown on herself, she realized with a pang. After a while, the lovely finery seemed pretty much the same. She ordered and selected what she knew the brides of Lover's Valley would find beautiful. Her reputation for creating a dream-come-true look brought hopeful brides to her shop from as far away as Oklahoma City.

But she'd never imagined a gown for herself. Getting married was a stressed-out affair, and she'd dressed enough brides to know it.

No, she had never locked the shop for the night, turned the lights in the main salon low and held gowns up to herself in front of a mirror. Once, a long time ago, she'd spent weeks choosing just the right prom dress and...it still hung in the attic in her family home, never danced in.

She frowned. Genie would be a challenge. "You're not as tall as me," she said, considering the delicate woman.

"Nope," Genie concurred cheerfully.

"You're quite tiny, actually," Crystal noted. "Petite."

"Right."

A great deal more willowy than her well-built brother, Crystal thought, before she quashed the memory of just how well-built Mitch had been even in high school. She swallowed, walking through her salon, lifting sleeves of gowns to consider the styles. "White?" she asked, realizing this could be an issue.

"Got any black? It would sure go better with my hair and not wash me out," Genie said hopefully.

Crystal let her breath out. Genie was right. White would make her ultra-porcelain features stand out terribly. And while raspberry-hued tresses and a lip ring weren't her choice of adornment, they were Genie's, and she needed to find a way to complement her. "I know this may sound totally way out, but it would not be terribly difficult to find a maid of honor gown in black. The color is very stylish now.''

''Oh, good.'' Genie's amethyst eyes lit up. ''I think that would be much more me.''

''What would you think about a short dress, which wouldn't be so overwhelming to your frame, and perhaps a large bouquet of elegant white flowers to soften the effect?''

Genie clasped her hands. ''Crystal, it sounds perfect!''

This was going better than she'd hoped. The joy of finding the just-right combination to please her customer flushed through her veins as it always did when everything fell into place. ''Come into a dressing room back here. I'll bring a couple of dresses for you to try so we can get the feel of the best silhouette for you, and then we'll look through some catalogs. And my shoes are probably too big for you, but you can slip into them so we can get a better idea of how the gowns would look,'' she said, thinking of the Birkenstock sandals Genie had left in the outer room.

''I'm getting so excited!'' Genie flashed to a dressing room to do her bidding. Crystal chose two short styles, one off-white because she didn't have it in black, and one in black that she knew would flatter Genie's small frame.

''It *is* exciting,'' she called absently. ''That's the way marriage should be.''

"Did you know my parents don't like my fiancé?"

Crystal's fingers stilled on the dress hooks she'd slid over the dressing room door. She didn't know what to say.

"I've been wondering if I'm just being radical," Genie confided. "I'm excited, but the other day I looked at myself in the mirror. I saw pink hair, a lip ring and a tattoo. I've always been kind of a rebel, you know?"

Crystal cleared her throat. "I suppose I'm just the opposite."

"Mitch says it's a by-product of being the baby in the family. He says I'm spoiled."

"Oh, my," Crystal murmured. "I'm sure you'd know whether you're in love. They say…I mean, I've heard it's like nothing else in the world." Her fingers twined together as embarrassment crept over her. Who was she to be handing out advice on love? This was an impossible assignment she'd agreed to. She couldn't counsel the sister of the one man she'd ever been wildly, innocently in love with.

A zipper rasped and Crystal stepped away from the door. "I'll wait for you in the outer salon."

"Okay."

Crystal breathed a sigh of relief and went into the main salon to wait.

The shop door swung open, sending the bells on the white velvet cord tinkling. Barney, Linc and Frankie strolled in. Swallowing a groan, she stared at the trio of ex-football players. "To what do I owe the honor of this visit?"

They all grinned. "We thought we'd stop by and talk you into going to dinner with us."

Crystal's eyebrows flew up. "Why?"

"'Cause we like you. Do you have something else you'd rather do than go out with three handsome guys?" Linc demanded.

She could hardly reply that she'd almost rather investigate lip-piercing techniques than go out with the three of them, but she was saved from answering.

"Wow!" Linc exclaimed as Genie appeared in the center of the salon.

The girl's features glowed from the emphasis of the black moiré against her pale skin and electric hair. For some reason, she'd removed her lip ring and touched her lips with bright pink lipstick. Crystal's shoes might have been a trifle too big, and the short evening gown could use a bit of tightening around Genie's gently slender body, but none of that seemed to matter to the suddenly gawking Linc. Genie seemed to enjoy the masculine attention, pirouetting to show off the low back of the dress.

"Do you like it?" she asked, her question apparently directed toward the shell-shocked Linc. "Would you marry me like this?"

"Would I?" He gave a low wolf whistle. "Let's fly to Nevada tonight!"

"Now, hang on a minute," Crystal interrupted,

fearing the conversation was getting out of hand. "Genie's already engaged to be married."

"Perhaps I was too hasty," Genie cooed. "Maybe I hadn't met my prince until now."

Crystal's eyes went wide. Surely they weren't serious with their flirting! She seated herself on a nearby sofa to stay out of the fast-blooming flirtation between the ex-jock and the black-gowned bride, just in case.

"We could discuss it over dinner," Linc enticed. "I know a cozy spot in a nearby town."

"Crystal, will you charge this dress to my brother's account?" Genie requested, slipping her arm through Linc's. "He said to listen to anything you suggested, and I most certainly have."

Crystal watched as Mitch's beaming little sister walked out with her bulging-biceped Romeo— wearing Crystal's black shoes. "Have a good time," she said weakly.

The door shut. She looked at Frankie and Barney in some astonishment.

"She did look pretty," Frankie said.

"She left me Birkenstocks to wear." Crystal stared at the worn brown footwear.

"Those are some unfortunate shoes," Barney said. "No wonder she snatched yours."

The shoes were the least of her problems. "Mitch is going to be furious. I was supposed to try to talk Genie out of getting married!"

"Oh, hell." Frankie slid the Birkenstocks over to her so she could put them on. "You're in the business of making dreams come true. You just did. Ring up the sale, put on the butt-ugly shoes, and we'll run you by your house to get something different before we go to dinner. You look like you could use a drink.''

"I could." Crystal locked up, slid her feet into the low-heeled, thick-soled shoes which did not complement her nine-to-five dress, and let Barney and Frankie escort her from the store. "Maybe I'm in the wrong business."

One on either side, they guided her across the street as if they feared she might repeat her fainting act.

"Once you find the right man to marry," Barney assured her, "you'll no longer be so frightened of true love striking you from out of nowhere."

"I'm not frightened!"

"Then make up your mind," Frankie instructed. "You'll never have a better selection than what is presently before you."

"About what? I make up my mind a hundred times a day." Crystal didn't think she should have to clarify that a businesswoman naturally made numerous decisions if she wanted to keep her customers happy and her business afloat.

"About which one of us you want," Barney told her. "The choices don't get any better than this!"

SHE SHOULD HAVE KNOWN Mitch would be waiting on her porch, Crystal thought as she walked up to her forest-green-and-glass front door. There was no question she wasn't living right, or she wouldn't be surrounded by three scowling men.

"I was coming to see how Genie's appointment went," Mitch said, frowning at the two large men flanking Crystal. He stared down at her horrible shoes. "Why are you wearing sandals like my sister's? You always wear conservative low heels."

"Not anymore," Crystal snapped. "Not since your sister waltzed off with my nice pumps." She went inside, and the hairy hounds burst out, barking at the men and sweeping themselves around Crystal's legs with joy.

"My sister took your shoes?"

"She needed them for her date with Linc," Barney explained.

Mitch's jaw dropped. "That's your idea of talking sense into my sister?"

Crystal turned, pressed all three men out onto the porch and blew a kiss they could split. "Good night, fellas."

She closed the door. Instant rapping exploded against the wood, but Crystal blithely walked around the front of the house, closing curtains and turning lamps low.

"Crystal!" Barney and Frankie hollered. "What about dinner?"

"Crystal!" Mitch called. "Please open the door!"

"There," Crystal said with a happy sigh as she melted into a fluffy chair in the parlor. "Just me and my pooches, cats and lovebirds, who never give me a moment's trouble.'' She patted furry noses and gazed at cats lining the mantel. ''Don't let all that noise outside upset you. From now on, this place is off-limits to disruptive males.''

The dogs thumped their tails. The knocking ceased at her door. She slipped off the Birkenstocks and sighed. ''You know, those are very comfortable shoes!''

THE NEXT TIME MITCH saw Crystal, it was early the next morning. She was sneaking up to his porch carrying his sister's shoes. He pulled open the door to get the newspaper and found her bending down to lay the shoes quietly on the mat.

''I was dropping off Genie's sandals. I'm on my way to work,'' she said hurriedly.

''Not without telling me what happened,'' he replied, pulling her into the house and closing the door. ''Join me for breakfast and give me the lowdown, because I think you owe me some kind of explanation.''

''No, I don't,'' Crystal declared. ''I never even discussed anything with Genie except dresses. I didn't invite Linc into the shop. Unless I'd had a crystal ball, I couldn't have foreseen any of what happened.''

She glared at him, and he glared back.

''Her fiancé is calling around here at the rate of once an hour to find her,'' Mitch said.

''That should make you happy. You didn't want her to marry him.''

"I didn't want her running off to Nevada last night, either," Mitch gritted out. "Especially not with a knucklehead like Linc." He checked his watch. "If my calculations are correct, at this moment I now have him for a brother-in-law!"

Crystal steeled herself not to laugh at the horror on Mitch's face. "I fail to see your objection. He hasn't been married numerous times. He has a great job. He's a nice man. He fell head over heels for Genie. It was like watching a mountain be toppled by a hummingbird." She crossed her arms. "So... would you like to first pay my bill for her dress, and then thank me for my assistance, as accidental as it was? Or vice versa?"

He grimaced at her teasing. "How much do I owe you?"

"Two hundred dollars. That includes tax."

Utter astonishment sent his eyebrows flying into his dark, nicely cut hair. "Two hundred dollars!"

"And that's not even including my shoes," Crystal said reasonably. "I'm only charging you for the dress, and giving you a slight discount at that since she didn't hang around long enough for alterations."

"How kind of you." His tone was sarcastic, but he snatched his billfold out of his jeans pocket and paid her with two one hundred dollar bills.

She smiled. "I'll put a receipt in the mail to you today. Do let me know if I can be of service again. And where I should send a wedding gift to the newlyweds."

Clearly the fact that his sister would be setting up house elsewhere hadn't set in, judging by the perplexed look on his face. But he bore up and nodded.

She walked to the door and waited for him to show her out.

He stood far back in the foyer, staring at her.

"What? What is it?" she asked.

"I'm just wondering," he said thoughtfully. "Wondering what it would be like if it was you and I who'd impulsively hopped a plane to Nevada."

"Oh, it would be very bad," Crystal said. "I'm a restless flier. I eat peanuts constantly. And drink Bloody Marys to keep myself calm."

"That bad, huh?"

"Oh, most definitely," she assured him. "You wouldn't enjoy flying with me at all." Without waiting for him to comment further, she opened the door and then, waving over her shoulder at him, quietly closed it.

He stared after her. His mother joined him in the foyer.

"Who was that?"

"Crystal. She was returning Genie's shoes."

"Did you tell her the good news?"

"If you could call it that." Mitch frowned. He wasn't sure what the desired outcome would have been, but Linc for a brother-in-law wouldn't have been in his top three choices.

"Couldn't she stay for breakfast?"

He shook his head. "She had to get to work."

His mother laughed. "She sure stays on the go."

True. Wherever he was, Crystal was sure to go away.

Flying wasn't all she seemed to fear. He wished easing that fear was as simple as wooing her with Bloody Marys and peanuts.

"FUNNY. I THOUGHT I JUST saw Crystal's car speed away from the McStern house." Uncle Martin checked his watch.

"Possibly she was dropping off a wedding gift," Bess suggested. "I hear that the McSterns are very pleased with their new son-in-law. Now they just have one more girl to get to the altar. Fortunately, they like that suitor."

"And what about Mitch?" Elle asked.

"Well, he's not engaged. I don't think they're worried about him." Bess began clearing the dishes. "I would think he'll head back to Dallas soon, now that the crisis with Genie has passed."

"Oh, dear," Elle murmured. "Remember your attack of conscience the other night?"

Bess arrested in midbend as she picked up plates. "What about it?"

"Perhaps you should confess before he leaves Lover's Valley," Elle suggested in a thin voice. "Who knows when he'll ever return?"

Bess swallowed, sliding into a chair. "I was thinking the same thing myself. I just don't want to."

Martin came over to pat her arm. "Why not?"

"Because…I'm scared," Bess whispered. "As selfish as it is, as cowardly as I know I am, I'm afraid my daughter might be so terribly angry with me she might never speak to me again!"

Elle got up to pat her sister's hand. "I understand completely, sister dear."

Bess swallowed. "If you two will excuse me, I think I'll go sit on the patio for a moment."

Bess quietly made her way to the great room, which opened onto the patio. Across a short path of large stepping stones was Elle's studio. Walking inside, she closed her eyes, sighing as she rubbed her chest. This was where she was most comfortable. In this room, her sister spent hours painting china with beautiful, dreamy patterns. She always felt the peace of serenity inside this room of Elle's romantic inspirations—but not today.

Reaching for the old-fashioned phone, she dialed a number from memory.

"Hello?"

She almost smiled with relief. "Mitch, it's Bess," she said softly.

"Hi, Bess. How are you doing?"

"Not too well, actually," she said, her voice a thin rasp. "I wonder if you could slip through the gate in back and visit me in Elle's studio? I don't want my sister and brother to know you're coming."

Mitch stared at the pasty-faced woman as he seated her on the floral chaise lounge inside a room filled with daintily painted objects. If it weren't for the fact that Bess was obviously ill, he would have wanted to take the time to leisurely admire the artist's work. "I don't understand. Why wouldn't you tell them you were in pain?"

"I didn't want to worry anyone," Bess said, her voice tight. "My chest has been bothering me on and off for a few days, since before Crystal's party. I didn't want to spoil it for her. She does so worry about me, you know."

Mitch gently took the thin, delicate fingers in his, feeling the crinkly skin and the somewhat moist palm. He frowned. Bess was in pain, hurting more than she cared to let anyone know. "I think you should see your doctor," he said, unobtrusively taking her pulse.

"I am," she replied, her breath shallow. "There's no one I trust more than you, Mitch." She turned to look at him. "You have no reason to trust us, but I've always known you were a good man. You were a good boy, and you turned out to make your parents proud."

"Rest," he told her. "Close your eyes and try to relax." He didn't have anything with him to assist him in diagnosing her complaint, but his immediate reaction was that she needed to be at a doctor's office at the minimum, and perhaps in a hospital. "I'm going to tell Elle and Martin that you need to see a doctor immediately."

"I am. You're the best there is, and make house calls, besides."

He nearly ground his teeth at her continued faith in him. Yes, he was a cardiac specialist, but he had none of her health history. Her regular doctor would know what medication she might be taking and be familiar with her history. "Bess," he said gently, "you must see your physician. He'll know best how to treat you."

She sighed. "He'll probably kill me, the old coot. But you do what you think is best."

He patted her hand. "Hang on. I'll go talk to Elle and Martin."

Turning her head, she met his gaze. The expression in her eyes was soft and grateful. "I know you still like my daughter, Mitch. I shouldn't have told you to stay away from her. Please forgive me. I mean well, but…"

She stopped speaking suddenly. Mitch wasn't certain if she was in greater pain or merely tired.

Without hesitating further, he hurried inside the main house.

Chapter Seven

Crystal stared at the larger-than-life woman taking up three square feet of her bridal salon. She was as tall as Mitch. She carried herself like Mitch.

She could not be called svelte.

"Mitch said you did a nice job with Genie. He thought maybe you could help me, too," Janet McStern said, her voice sweet and unsure.

Crystal hadn't seen Janet in years, but this was not how she remembered her. Janet had always been more like Mitch in frame, but not overweight. Nor so uncertain.

And though business was business and couldn't be sniffed at, Crystal had to wonder at the real reason behind Mitch sending his other sister to her shop. "I understand Mitch really likes your fiancé, Janet," she said carefully as she motioned for her to take a seat on the sofa. She wanted a chance to chat with her about her wishes for her dream wedding—clearly petite, funky Genie couldn't be used as a guide. Janet had lovely chestnut hair and dark blue eyes. She had a tiny nose set above finely drawn lips that carried tiny dimples beside them, as if she was a woman who loved to smile and laugh—ordinarily.

"All my family loves him," Janet said warmly. Her expressive eyebrows rose under delicate bangs, lovely hair that Crystal thought only needed an up-sweep to maximize her fabulous eyes.

Like her brother's.

They could pick out a lovely, understated veil to attach to a pretty chignon, and voilà—

"Can I ask you something, Crystal?" Janet asked.

"Sure." Her mind was on the type of gown that might most flatter Janet's nicely healthy figure. In a magazine she'd recently seen a stunning lace over satin—

"Why haven't you married?"

Crystal's mind snapped back to the salon. What an awkward question coming from Mitch's sister! "I haven't met the man of my dreams," she hedged. That was the truth, wasn't it? She hadn't in the last decade, anyway.

"Oh."

Janet crossed her legs at the ankles and Crystal noted the high-heeled red shoes she wore. Obviously, the fiancé was tall enough for Janet to wear those shoes, and that was a good sign. Crystal could have a wide choice of shoe styles to suggest Janet choose. She liked the fact that Janet didn't feel the need to dress down because of her weight.

"I'm not sure I've met the man of my dreams,

either,'' Janet said. Her voice was casual, but the look in her eyes was not. It was edgy, and distressed. Somehow heartbroken.

Crystal's pulse picked up rapidly, too rapidly. *Drat! I should have known there was a hook in this fairy tale!*

Gently, she closed the book of wedding fashions she'd placed on the sofa between them. Janet hadn't bothered to so much as pick the book up. ''I don't know what to say, Janet.''

Her sweet face rounded with an embarrassed smile. ''I'm hoping you'll tell me I simply have wedding jitters. That you see this all the time in your shop, and that all brides get them.''

Crystal's heart ached for Janet. ''I'm sorry. I see a lot of nerves. There's more anxiety between these four walls sometimes than a shrink probably sees in a year. Butterflies are very common, but I sense that you're talking about doubt, not wedding bell panic.''

Janet's smile was sad. ''He's such a nice man.''

''Oh, dear.'' Crystal reached for a tissue box and pulled one out for herself before thinking to hand one to Janet. What an unfortunate spot for Janet to be in! She could sympathize with her dilemma. ''I'm so sorry.''

''I don't know how to tell my family,'' she said softly. ''They're crazy about him. They'll think I'm nuts to let him go. And my friends will, too. I know they'll say I'm lucky to have him, considering my size, but—''

"Don't let anyone say that to you. That's ridiculous!" Crystal's back went up and the urge to cry left her instantly. "You shouldn't get married just because someone will take you even though you're not in current weight fashion. You should get married because you're in love with him and he's in love with you!"

"Good men are hard to find."

"That's why you should enjoy the good ones when you meet them, but marry the one who doesn't make you feel like he's doing you a favor. Or like you have to marry him because you might never get a second chance. It's supposed to be a partnership of equals. You should feel beautiful and accepted on your wedding day."

"I've been so worried lately that I've been eating like a herd of wild horses." Janet's cheeks turned pink, her skin dewy.

"I thought maybe you didn't seem quite your old self," Crystal softly said. "I love cheesecake when I'm upset. And I don't mean just one or two slivers. I mean I love the entire thing, and I'm not picky about the flavor."

Janet laughed. "Mitch was right."

"About what?" Crystal felt a frown coming on. She wasn't going to agree that Mitch was right about anything until she knew exactly what it was.

"He said you could help, and he was right."

"I don't think this was the kind of help he meant."

"No," Janet said with a smile. "Especially not

since he told me that you'd help me find just the right dress.'' She reached over to clasp Crystal's hand. ''Thank you so much for helping me find the right attitude instead. I've been so panicked and worried wondering if I was a fool to break off an engagement. You've given me an immeasurable gift. And I really do appreciate it.''

''You're welcome.'' She got up to walk Janet to the door of the salon.

''I'll be back when I've met the right man.''

''I hope so.'' Crystal tried to smile. ''I'd like to meet him.''

Janet smiled and started to walk out. Suddenly she turned around. ''Can I ask you one more thing?''

''Of course.''

''Do you *want* to meet the man of your dreams?''

''Um, no. There seems to be an unwritten rule that if you work in a bridal salon, you have little time for dreaming of your own wedding.'' *There. Nice cover, Crystal.*

''That's too bad.'' Janet shook her head. ''I always hoped you and Mitch would get back together. So do Mom and Dad. For that matter,'' she continued, ''I noticed Mitch sure does talk about you a lot these days.'' She shrugged. ''Oh, well. One thing I've learned is that if something's not meant to be, it's not meant to be. Bye, Crystal, and thanks again.''

''You're welcome.'' Crystal shut the door and went to sink down onto the sofa. *Great.* Mitch was going to breathe fire when he learned that she'd been instrumental in helping Janet to break an engagement of which his family approved!

Tough luck. Janet hadn't been happy. If Crystal had to explain that fact to Mitch, she would.

Fortunately, he was out of sisters. There were no more he could send to her shop. No more relationships she could unwittingly send in a different direction than what he anticipated.

She sighed with relief.

The next time the door opened, Mitch walked in. Crystal stiffened into a formal sitting position.

"Elle and Martin ran your mother over to the doctor this morning," he told her. "They just called my cell phone to say that she's being taken to a hospital outside of Dallas." His eyes softened on her. "If you can put a sign up in the window saying you'll be gone for a couple of hours, I'll drive you over. I think they're not going to waste any time addressing the situation."

"Oh, my gosh!" Crystal jumped to her feet, her hands shaking as she scribbled a quick sign to stick in the window. She turned off the lights and Mitch held the door open for her. "I can take my own car," she said, her heart feeling like it was beating painfully in her throat.

"I'll drive you," he said, without room for argument. "You had a fainting spell when you panicked the other day. I don't want you to get hurt," he said gruffly.

"I did not panic!" She followed him, her ire already flaming to the surface. "I...I was shaken."

"And you're shaken now." He took her by the arm to lead her to the car he'd parked in front. "By the way, I suggested that my sister Janet come by sometime today and have you help her pick out a dress for her wedding." He slid into the driver's seat and switched the Mercedes on. "She's engaged to a great guy, a surgeon buddy of mine. He's really top-notch in the field of—"

"Mitch."

He glanced at her, his monologue halting. "What?"

"Why are you talking so fast?" She eyed him. "You seem uncharacteristically anxious."

"I'm not." He kept his gaze on the road, though they sat at a two-stop intersection and the only traffic around was an old dog sunning himself in the dirt between the road and the shops.

"Is there more wrong with Mom than what you're telling me?" Crystal's stomach tightened uncomfortably.

"I don't know much more than I've told you. I had Elle and Martin take her to her physician, and they've just called me. We'll find out more when we see them."

Crystal's eyes grew wide. "Why did you have them take her to the doctor?"

He drove down the street none too slowly, his hands firm on the steering wheel.

But not relaxed.

"Bess called me over. She wanted me to tell her what was wrong. Apparently, she hasn't been feeling quite herself for a while."

"I didn't know that!" Anguish tore through Crystal.

"Neither did anyone else." He turned his head to look at her. "Are you all right?"

"I'm fine," she murmured. "Thank you, Mitch, for coming to pick me up." And then she sat back in the seat to wait until they arrived at the hospital, her heart palpitating, her hands trembling.

THE FIRST PERSON they ran into at the hospital was Janet's ex-fiancé. Crystal knew this in the first few seconds of introduction. Mitch greeted the fellow physician as if he was his best friend in the world, shaking his hand with enthusiasm and grinning with pleasure.

The doctor held back a little stiffly in the handshake.

"Crystal!" Mitch exclaimed. "I'd like you to meet Hiram Hensley, one of my great friends, an excellent surgeon and my sister Janet's fiancé!"

Crystal smiled—just enough to make her face feel like it was cracking. Before she could say how do you do, Hiram turned a jaundiced eye on her.

"I feel as though I've already met you," Hiram said. "I believe Janet was in your bridal salon this morning. You gave her some advice."

Crystal gulped, her gaze jumping with guilt-speed to Mitch's happy face.

"Oh, Janet was already *in* your store," he said. "You didn't tell me that, Crystal!" Mitch held her closely to his side as if she were a good friend—or better. "I sent Janet over to get the prettiest wedding gown she could buy, Hiram. Crystal's just the person to fix her right up."

"She certainly did that." Hiram leveled a rather pained expression on Crystal. "If you'll excuse me, I have a young patient waiting. Pea gravel in nose. Can't be blown out or dislodged and may require my services. Goodbye, Mitch. Crystal." He swept her with her gaze. "I'd like to say that it was a pleasure to meet you, but under the circumstances…"

The tall, silver-haired doctor walked away. Mitch's mouth hung open as he whipped around to stare at Crystal. "What was *that* all about?"

"Oh, dear. Mitch, listen. Let's talk about this later, okay? I really need to see Mother." She started to walk away, then decided she was perhaps being selfish. After all, Mitch was trying to help her family. He'd done a lot for them. She reminded herself of this again and slowly turned around. "When Janet came to see me this morning, she was upset."

"About Hiram?"

He was clearly in water too deep, Crystal saw. "About the wedding," she said softly. "I think that's why Janet procrastinated about buying a gown. Maybe accepting Hiram's proposal seemed like a good idea in the first place, but after a while,

your sister realized she wasn't in love with him."
Crystal reached out to touch Mitch's sleeve. "I'm
sorry."

"You're sorry?" He looked like the breath had
been knocked out of him. "You're *sorry?*" He
glanced after his friend, who'd walked through
some double doors. "Janet wasn't upset about getting married *until* she walked into your shop." For
a moment, he stood helplessly, his hands at his
sides. "I know what it is. You're trying to get back
at me for not showing up prom night. You've deliberately ruined both my sisters' chances of happiness to pay me back."

Crystal's eyebrows rose. "What an idiotic thing
to say. Excuse me. I'm going to find Mother."

She turned and he lightly caught her hand.
"Deny it."

"I just did. I only deny stupid accusations once.
You're upset. I'm sorry your good buddy isn't going to become your brother-in-law, at least not in
the near future. But I'm not a vengeful person,
Mitch. Once upon a time, you knew me better than
I knew myself. Clearly, we don't know each other
at all anymore."

She snatched her hand away from him and
marched herself over to the nurses' desk. "Can you
tell me what room Bess Jennings is in, please?"

The candy striper looked at the computer.
"Room 101 in the cardiac wing. That's a temporary
room, but you can catch her there now."

"Thank you." Crystal hurried to the elevator bank, aware that Mitch followed.

They got on the elevator together. The doors slid shut.

"I'm sorry," he said. "To say that I was shocked is mild."

"Fine." She prayed as the elevator ground to a sudden stop. The doors didn't open. Her gaze stayed glued to the lit number.

"We stopped between floors," Mitch said, punching the buttons again.

Crystal told herself not to worry. Between ground floor and the first floor was safe enough. She wouldn't have to climb out very far.

Mitch shook his head. "This hospital is so old it must have gremlins in the elevators. Somebody will be along shortly and notice it's not moving."

"Use the phone," Crystal instructed edgily.

"I tried. It's dead." He looked at her, and Crystal was suddenly aware that this was the last place on earth she'd ever want to be, stuck with a man she'd tried for thirteen years to forget. She thought about how he'd kissed her the other day and felt her knees go weak. She thought about him accusing her of messing up his sisters' lives, and though he'd apologized, it showed he knew nothing about her at all. Or Janet and Genie, for that matter.

Her feelings were more than hurt that he'd lashed out at her that way. Crystal folded her arms, leaned against the wall and prayed that the elevator would move soon.

She did not want to be stuck with Mitch. Barney or Frankie she could handle, but this... Out of the corner of her eye, she took in Mitch's tight jeans, fitted blue polo shirt, soft ebony hair and somehow cute frown as he stared into the elevator box.

No. Being stranded in an elevator with a man that good-looking was a shame if you didn't like him.

And I definitely don't like him.

He sighed and turned to face her. "I suppose while we're in here I should tell you something your mother said to me."

She raised her eyebrows but didn't comment.

"Now, keep in mind she was in pain, so she wasn't thinking straight," Mitch told her.

Her heart seemed to halt in her chest. "How much pain? What is wrong with her?"

"No one will know until they run the appropriate tests, Crystal. I don't have access to her records, so I couldn't begin to make a guess, other than her heart rhythm seemed to be a bit uneven. And she complained of some soreness in her arm that concerned me. But I'd rather leave the speculating to the doctors in charge. Right now, my concern, since we're here for a couple of minutes, out of anyone's range of vision, is imparting to you something odd she mentioned to me."

"Go ahead."

He seemed unprepared to force the words from his mouth. Glancing away, he scratched his head. Then he looked up at the unlit numbers as if hoping for an immediate resurgence of power. His lips compressed for a second. "Yourmomwantsmeto-marryyou."

"I beg your pardon?" Crystal leaned forward a little so that she could hear better. "Could you say that more slowly? I couldn't decode a word."

His face turned a bit red. He scratched at his neck above the jersey polo collar. "Your...mom...wants...me...to...marry...you."

Crystal made a sucking noise of exasperation. "Ridiculous," she said. "And pathetic."

The number lights turned on, the elevator wheezed, and it jerked to the first floor. The doors opened magically.

She stepped out, breathing circulated air and the smell of disinfectant. "My mother has always had a vivid imagination," she said, turning to face him. "No doubt being ill has accelerated that somehow. I apologize for the awkward position she has placed you in. You must believe me when I tell you that, although they may have been hunting a man most fiercely for me when they pulled you into my store, I do not want to get married. You're safe. So let's agree to do one thing in tandem, Mitch. If she brings it up again, we'll both gently tell her no. All right?"

Without waiting for his reply, Crystal strode to her mother's room.

Chapter Eight

"I am actually quite afraid," Bess admitted.

"Mom, it's going to be fine." Crystal felt none of the calm she tried to impart but she refused to show her own fear.

Her mother reached out and clutched Crystal's hand. "I'm not trying to be pessimistic, but what if the balloon procedure doesn't work? What if it's more serious than that?"

"Oh, Mom. You're much too strong for anything to get you down for long." Crystal sat on the edge of the bed and held her mother's hand more tightly.

Mitch sat and took Bess's other hand. "You'll be in the best of hands."

She shook her head, her stubborn streak clearly at the fore. "I wouldn't be lying here if I didn't have a guilty conscience."

"You wouldn't be lying here if you hadn't over-worked yourself on my birthday party." Crystal leaned to kiss her mother's forehead. "As much as I enjoyed the party, I think you must have over-done."

"Nonsense." Bess impatiently pulled her hands back. "My conscience is my downfall. One's skeletons always pop out of the closet eventually. Usually when it's most inconvenient."

Crystal didn't want to think about skeletons. She had enough of her own to rattle her conscience. Hesitantly, she glanced at Mitch, but he was completely focused on her mother.

"We hear lots of deathbed confessions," he said, his eyes twinkling with mischief. "You're not on yours, so you can save your confession for another time."

Bess compressed her lips belligerently. "You just don't want to hear my confession," she accused Mitch. "Have you thought about what I told you?"

"Mom, please. You're distressing yourself more. Anything that may be troubling you is insignificant right now. Just rest."

"I can't." Bess eased herself up on her pillow, her face strained with worry. "It concerns both of you and I'd like you to listen."

Mitch and Crystal glanced at each other. "I sincerely wish Aunt Elle hadn't pulled you inside my store," Crystal said to him. "Ever since you reappeared in my well-ordered life, utter turmoil has visited us like a plague."

He grinned at her. "Your mother's trying to confess. You're interrupting. Trying to grab the spotlight."

"Oh, brother," Crystal said impatiently. "If it

will make you feel better, Mother, we are listening, although I am positive you are making yourself ill over nothing. We will hear this confession, and then you will have your surgery, you will be well, and we will put this whole problem behind us. All right?'' She sent a glare Mitch's way so he couldn't possibly misunderstand her meaning. A shrug and way-too-confident grin was all she got for her efforts.

He had never been light on the irresistible scale. What woman wouldn't be flattered by his unshakable interest in her?

And somehow, having Mitch with her right now was very comforting. Though she kept up a brisk front rather than risk panicked tears, she was very, very frightened about her mother's coronary condition. He squeezed her hand suddenly, and Crystal felt a shock go all the way through her.

She pulled her hand away. The problem was, counting on Mitch had cost her once before. Allowing herself to depend upon him too much could leave her hanging in the breeze emotionally again. ''I must admit to being curious now,'' she told her mother, making certain the glance she gave Mitch was cool.

Bess shot her a look Crystal couldn't decipher. She wanted to see slyness. She wanted to see a glint of intrepid triumph.

But all she saw in her mother's eyes was sadness. And apprehension.

Instantly she knew her mother believed every

word she was about to say. And somehow it boded ill for Crystal.

"Whatever you think you did," Crystal said softly, gently twining her fingers through Bess's, "it's in the past. I would rather it stay there. I'm certain Mitch would, too. It isn't going to change anything for either of us at this point. It's just upsetting you needlessly. Don't you agree, Mitch?"

"I don't know. Confession is supposed to be great for the soul. Unload, Bess."

Crystal wanted to smack him for his smarmy attitude. Couldn't he see the worst possible thing for her mother right now was more anxiety? "Is that how you advise your patients? Unload?"

"For most patients I couch it in more specific terms. Let it all hang out, let it rip, shout till it's out, scream…"

"I'm going to scream if you two don't stop bickering." Bess gave them equal glares. She took a deep breath. "The day of the prom Kathryn came by the house looking for Crystal. You were not home," she said to her daughter, jumping into her confession most ungracefully. "I could see she was frantic. I invited her in for a cup of tea. She sat at my table, and as Mitch so eloquently prescribes, let it all hang out. She was pregnant and she had been dumped by her boyfriend. As you know, she was one of the girls nominated for prom queen."

"I know. I voted for her," Crystal said miserably. "She was my best friend." Not after that night, of course. They'd never spoken again, except for cool hellos, until Crystal's birthday party.

"She could not go to the prom without a date," Bess continued. She stopped speaking for a moment, emotional pain showing in her eyes. "You had come in late the night before, Crystal."

In that second, Crystal knew that her and Mitch's guilty secret had never really been a secret. She held in a humiliated breath. All these years, her mother had known—and never voiced a word of condemnation.

"What can I say? I couldn't bear the thought of you ending up in the same position as Kathryn. You were very young. All of you. I was certain you'd get over it."

That pronouncement left the three of them sitting quietly, awkwardly. Crystal couldn't bear to look at Mitch, or her mother. Crossing her legs at the ankles, she stared at the navy blue silk covering her lap. *Why did I wear such a dark color today?* she thought irrationally. *I should have dressed in something optimistic, like hot pink.*

Maybe that's why she'd never envisioned herself wearing one of her own gowns. Optimism was a trait she undervalued, and with good reason.

She stood. "If you're trying to say that you somehow are behind Mitch not showing up for our date, I can only say that he certainly didn't mind his dates being switched." He'd kissed Kathryn, and that didn't speak to a heartbroken condition. She leaned down to kiss her mother's forehead. "I have to go feed my pets and let them outside. Please rest until the nurses come and get you for surgery. Aunt Elle and Uncle Martin will be here soon, and I'll be here when you wake up.''

She turned and practically ran from the room.

Bess stared at Mitch. ''It's really you I need to talk to now.''

He shook his head ruefully. ''You're working at full speed. I'll never be able to get this whole thing straightened out with Crystal.''

''I know it won't be easy. But Mitch, whether you know it or not, I did you both a huge favor. At least, I thought I did. You both had a chance to get out into the world and prove yourselves. Young love would never have lasted through the stress of college and med school and everything else. You and Crystal deserved to see some of the world without being held back.''

''That sounds like rationalization.''

She tapped him on the wrist. ''It wouldn't have lasted then, but there's every chance it could now.''

''I don't know. She's pretty determined not to give me a shot.''

''Crystal has a right to be mad, but now that she knows I had some hand in it, maybe she'll be a bit more forgiving. Especially once she knows the whole story.''

''I don't give it much hope.''

''I want you to talk to her. In fact, I want you to propose to her quite seriously. Make her understand how much you care for her. For my sake.'' She drew a deep breath. "I know you care for her. And she cares for you. You two were never good at hiding anything."

He grinned. "Would an engagement between us make you happy?"

"Absolutely. I could die happy then."

Reaching over, he tweaked her cheek. "You're not dying."

"Maybe not, but there are some goals I haven't achieved in my life, and I'd like to do it before I am on my deathbed. Such as grandchildren."

"Oh, I see."

"Seventeen was too young. But Crystal's thirty and that's just about right," Bess said with satisfaction. "I'm sure she wants children."

He laughed out loud. She eyed him distrustfully.

"Since I am on my deathbed, and since I have gone to the trouble of confessing my ill deed, the two of you getting back together would be the perfect ending to the matter," she insisted. "She's never gotten over you," she said more softly. "Surely a mother is allowed one last machination in her life?"

"We're talking about Crystal here," he reminded her. "I don't think there's much motivation for her to marry me, machination or no."

"Well, I can't do everything for you, Mitch McStern! That one you'll have to work out on your own."

He covered her hand with his. "I'll see what I can do."

"What I wish you'd do is perform this surgery," she said irritably. "I really am frightened out of my wits."

"You need to follow your doctor's suggestions," he said gently. "And besides, I'll need my full attention if I'm to win Crystal over, right?"

She didn't look convinced. "You're just cosseting me because I'm scared. I don't think you have any intention at all of convincing Crystal to marry you. I just know she'd say yes, once she gets over her pride."

Mitch smiled. Crystal was more complicated than that. The part of the story Bess had unloaded was small compared to the whole. He wasn't certain Crystal hadn't built up enough wall between them to keep him from ever breaking through the fortress.

He'd have to do it brick by brick.

"I was kind of hoping you'd ask her soon," Bess said, her voice tired and weak. "If Crystal's wearing an engagement ring by the time I wake up, I just know my recovery would go much smoother. I might actually live."

She closed her eyes. Mitch started to make a standard teasing remark, then held it back. Silently, he stroked her wrist.

Doctor to patient, he realized she really believed she was on her deathbed, or approaching it. And that she was paying the price for what she'd done all those years ago. Somehow, fear had mixed into her guilt and made a powerful cocktail of foreboding.

He sighed, put her hand gently on her abdomen and decided to pay a visit to Crystal.

For Bess's sake—and his own.

WHEN CRYSTAL OPENED the door, Mitch could tell she'd been crying. He could also tell she'd been using the dogs as tissues because their coats were moist and she had a few pieces of collie fur stuck to her wet cheek. "How about a sleeve instead?" he asked, and held up his arm.

To his shock, she came into his arms and burst into tears against his chest.

His eyebrows shot up. Crystal sobbed against his chest, and Mitch decided he kind of liked being a human tissue. "Let me take you inside," he suggested softly, maneuvering her around shaggy bodies. He closed the door with his foot and took her to the overstuffed sofa. "Did I ever tell you that you look beautiful in fur?" he asked her.

"Oh, Mitch." She stopped crying on a laugh, accepted a tissue he swiped from the end table but kept her head against his shoulder. "Do you ever say anything serious during a serious situation?"

"Probably not," he said, stroking her back, manfully ignoring the urge to trace her bra strap. He'd been able to undo Crystal's bra with one hand, a feat of which he'd been enormously proud as a teenager. He suspected he could still do it, and that her breasts were still as sweet and pliable as they'd been before. He tried to push that memory aside. "It's part of my bedside manner to treat serious situations with some levity. Laughter is the best medicine, you know. That and a healthy dose of prayer is the secret to my success."

She smiled and wiped mascara from under her eyes. "I'm not a cardiac patient, so you can quit being a comedian."

He sighed and leaned back against the sofa. "I'll try. Why are you crying? Your mother or your mother?"

"My mother, and you're not trying very hard to be serious," she mock scolded. "She's got me upset with all her deathbed talk. Choosing now to confess doesn't reassure me. And I would rather not have known."

"Prefer to see me as the villain, do you?"

"Yes." She gave him a sidelong glance. "I do. You are, no matter how much Mother tries to paint you with a white hat. She's just trying to get me married off, and she's not above fitting us together any way she has to." She shook her head at him, her smile disappearing. "Isn't that the most awful thought?"

He didn't think so, and it irritated him that she did. "I like the idea of being married to you."

She gazed at him, her expression unsure.

"In fact, I came over here to propose to you." He glanced down at the three dogs at his feet eyeing him steadily. "Do I have to ask them for your hand in marriage?"

She got up and shooed all the pets out into the backyard. Closing the door, she turned to look at him. "Mitch, I wouldn't marry you if you were the last man on earth. You went out with my best friend and dumped me. I know the circumstances were dire and I'm sure everyone acted as nobly as possible considering, but I could never trust you to be there for me, no matter what. Your personality is too easygoing, you don't have a serious bone in your body except when it comes to your sisters' choice of husbands, and you and I have nothing in common anymore." She went into the kitchen, so he followed, watching as she took down a hand-painted teacup. Silently, she made tea, finding a mug in the cupboard that had a picture of a collie on it for him. He sat at the kitchen table, his gaze on her behind as she worked at the stove.

"We have past history," he said softly. "We're from the same place."

"Then I could marry Frankie or Barney. In fact, Barney wants to marry me and then I'd still make my mother happy." She perked up, swiveling to face him. "Barney understands just what kind of marriage I need, too. This may be the best plan yet. I make my mother happy so she can heal because her only daughter is married, and yet I rebel in one tiny sense by not marrying the man she's recently handpicked for me."

"I don't like the thought of you rebelling," he said morosely. "I'm pretty sure you should listen to your mother. I've heard mothers know best."

"But," Crystal said triumphantly, "she didn't know best prom night, did she? She thought she did, but even she admitted she messed up."

He scratched his head. "She may have known best, Crystal. And I'm finding it difficult to see you with Barney."

"You won't have to. I'll keep the curtains closed."

His mouth dropped open as she handed him the mug of steaming tea. "You're not serious."

"If my being married will help Mother get better, I most certainly am serious." Crystal sat at the table, her expression sublime. "I see Barney in a charcoal-gray tux with long tails, don't you?"

He banged his mug down onto the wooden surface of the table, sloshing tea. "Crystal, you are one hardhearted lady. Did you know that? And as a physician who certainly understands the ins and outs of the mitral valves and every other function of the organ, I am certainly baffled by yours."

She smiled at him with mischievous delight. "I really don't want to get married. Some women don't. Look at your sister, for example. Your expectations nearly forced Janet into a miserable marriage."

"She's the one who said yes, for crying out loud! I wasn't even in the room when Hiram proposed!"

"Yes, but when Janet had second thoughts, she was afraid to call it off because she knew how upset you'd be. And she was right."

"I still think you had a big hand in that. You

could have convinced her that marriage to a smart, well-respected doctor was a good thing. Instead, you encouraged her to give one of my peers the boot!'' He glared at her. ''In fact, I'm still upset with you about that. How many women pass up a man like Hiram?''

''I would,'' she said softly. ''I would pass up a smart, well-respected doctor if I didn't love him.''

He drummed his fingers on the table. After a moment, he said, ''What did you mean when you said that Barney understood what you needed?''

''Well,'' she said thoughtfully, setting her teacup across from his mug, ''he suggested that we get married because we both really want to be left alone. He wants to keep hanging out with the guys, and I don't want all the fuss and bother of...''

''Of?'' he prompted.

''Of falling in love. It's messy,'' she said hurriedly. ''I don't want to think about sad things. I want to always focus on dreams and fantasy. My wedding boutique allows me to vicariously live the good part of other's people's lives. If I could handle distress and reality, I'd be a divorce lawyer. I don't want to be divorced.''

''You're not even married yet, Crystal. Why do you assume you'd be divorced?''

''I don't know.'' She laced her fingers together and leaned away from him, her eyes down. ''I don't want to...I don't want to...you know. Find out a man doesn't love me again.''

The earth fell away from his feet. "Is that what you thought?"

She looked at him, her eyes sparkling again with unshed tears. "It's what I knew for many years. That you had fallen out of love with me after we made love. I believed you had left me for a prettier, more popular girl. And no matter how much Mother tries to fix the situation now, nothing can erase all the years I thought no man would want me for the long term. It was empty. It was lonely. It was devastating, and I don't ever want to go there again."

Chapter Nine

Mitch swallowed. He wanted to touch Crystal, to tuck her hair behind her ear, but he knew beyond a shadow of a doubt that was the last thing she wanted. Even if her mother had been trying to erase the past, it stood between them more firmly than ever. "So you'd rather have a marriage of convenience with Barney than risk your heart again?"

"I'd never given it much thought before, but yes, I would much prefer to go into something with my eyes open than to face the unknown. Barney's pretty predictable. Though if you want the whole truth, I'd rather stick a straight pin in my eye than get married at all."

He shook his head. "You're so cynical! And to think I sent my sisters to you for advice. No wonder nothing went the way I planned it."

She shrugged. "Sorry. Well, no, I'm not sorry, because they're both happier now. I do make other women's dreams come true, Mitch, even if it isn't by way of the average method. However, having dressed enough stressed-out brides to last a lifetime,

I fail to see what the attraction is to getting married. I think half of them go to the altar just so they can have the gown of their dreams. But I don't think it's always about the man of their dreams."

"Crystal! You don't believe in romance!"

She stiffened. "What's your point?"

"You're Sister Scrooge of Wedded Bliss! How can you run a bridal shop and be such a nonbeliever?"

A frown traced her lips. "I have bills to pay, Mitch, just like everyone else. Lover's Valley needed a bridal shop. I provided it, and the stuff of dreams turned into green in my bank account. Why am I cynical? In a man it would be called sharp business acumen."

He drummed the table again, his lips twisting as he considered her words. "Okay. Say I concede your point."

"That your sisters are happier since I assisted them? Or that marriage is an overrated method of achieving happiness?"

"No—all right. All of the above, and that a marriage of convenience has its benefits."

She looked surprised. "Are you offering your support if I married Barney?"

"No, I'm offering you a marriage of convenience to me. I'm proposing it, in fact."

Once the words were out, Mitch couldn't call them back, and he could almost see them hanging over the table as Crystal tried to digest what he'd said.

"I don't think you're a marriage-of-convenience kind of guy," Crystal objected. "Your way of looking at women is different from Barney's. As I recall, you're a conquer-and-possess kind of man. All or nothing. I'm not sure laissez-faire extends that far into your personality."

"It might. It does, as a matter of fact. I can compromise just as well as the next man, Crystal."

He could tell by the suspicious look on her face that she wasn't buying his story. Incentive was needed. "Your mother's surgery is this afternoon. It's a fairly routine procedure, but she's understandably worried. She wants to know her daughter will be taken care of after she's gone, not financially, of course, because you're doing well on your own, but emotionally. I would always be there for you, Crystal."

Crystal closed her eyes, her heart pounding in her chest. It felt as if she was about to suffer a real panic attack of her own. She was too young for a hot flash and too healthy for a heart attack, but she had a weakness for Mitch and it manifested itself into going loose-limbed.

She clung to the table with one hand and told herself to breathe deeply. "You don't make me feel secure, Mitch. You make me short of respiration."

"That could be a serious condition. Maybe I should listen to your chest."

She shook her head at him in the negative. "I let you play premed student with me too many times for my own health. I believe I'll pass."

"But look how that experience paid off. I couldn't have made it without you. And if we'd made love more than once, Crystal, I probably would have become a gynecologist."

"A specialty to which you would no doubt have been admirably suited." Her chest lightened, and her breathing returned to normal. It was difficult to take Mitch too seriously when he was in his normal bedside manner, and she was beginning to think she preferred him this way. When he was earnest and she could see what reminded her of his love in his eyes, she felt panicky and nervous.

Nerves did not suit a woman who ran a bridal shop. She had to be in control for all the brides who suffered nerves.

Now she knew why they did. Throwing yourself out on a limb without anything under that limb except open, black space was decidedly terrifying. "I don't think I could make it to the altar with you, even under convenient terms," she told him. "Something still tells me Barney is safer."

"Let me call him," Mitch said, getting to his feet. "I'm pretty sure there's a chink in his armor you haven't seen yet. Barney and I should get equal time in your decision."

"I haven't decided to decide!" Crystal protested. She jumped up to place her hand over the phone so he couldn't pick it up.

"I wish you would," he said softly, pulling her up against him so that her heart pounded all over again. "I want you to pick me so badly it hurts,

Crystal. Physician heal thyself doesn't work with me, because you're the only medicine I want.''

He put his lips against hers in a kiss that sent Crystal spinning into tomorrow, and the last thing she thought before he swept her up into his arms was *this time I won't hit the floor.*

It felt like heaven to be in his arms again.

Mitch wasn't certain when he realized he was going to make love to Crystal. He only knew when she went soft in his arms that she had surrendered, and she had been oh, so right about him being an all-or-nothing kind of guy. He wanted her bad—he wanted her more than anything he'd ever wanted in his life. Desire pulled taut within him, a lifeline that had never severed no matter how many years had passed, and when he buried himself inside her and reveled at her cry of pleasure, it never crossed his mind to point out that he could still undo her bra with one hand.

WHEN CRYSTAL AWAKENED, the dogs were barking their summons for supper. Mitch leaned up on one elbow and grinned down at her.

Her heart started pounding painfully, and her stomach clutched as if she had rocks rolling around inside her.

''I've compromised you,'' he said, ''and I enjoyed every moment of it. I am immediately restating my offer of a marriage of convenience. I do not want you to ever think again that I have made love to you and then dumped you. Marry me, Crystal Star Jennings.''

She raised an eyebrow. ''You are not a marriage-of-convenience kind of man. Stop trying to kid yourself.''

''I can change.''

She got out of bed and pulled the sheet with her to avoid Mitch's appreciative eye. This left him exposed to her vision but he didn't reach for the bedspread. No modesty, of course.

And Crystal had to admit, Mitch without modesty was a darn heartstopping sight. ''I'm going to feed the animals.''

''I'll help.'' He hopped to his feet. ''Share your sheet with me. Everything's better when it's shared, chores included.''

He wrapped himself up in the trailing end of the sheet, winding himself as close to her body as he could so that they stood tightly together.

''I feel like a wonton,'' she said, but her protest was mild. Mitch's body through the sheet was strong and hard, and she was beginning to get a craving for him and maybe some Chinese food.

''Maybe we should get some takeout for your mom,'' he suggested as they waddled toward the back door, ''when she's home and recovering. Chinese food is remarkably calming. And fortune cookies are always amusing. Bess needs some laughter in her life.''

His groin bumped up against her bottom as she bent over, and Crystal immediately straightened.

"Is this necessary?" she complained as her craving for something other than takeout intensified. Something in the sheet felt like it was becoming shaped like a spring roll—something other than Chinese food appeared to be on Mitch's mind as well. She wasn't prepared for an ongoing sexual relationship with Mitch. "Truly, I can do this by myself."

"In a marriage of convenience, I think we split everything fifty-fifty. Right?"

"Not necessarily the sheets. Give me some room." She sighed, bending again to reach the large canister of dog food. Mitch bent with her. The dogs ignored the two-headed preparation of their supper as they waited for their bowls to be filled. "I'm trying to envision myself wadded up in a sheet with Barney."

"Well, don't." Mitch moved toward the back door to return inside, and Crystal had no choice but to follow. "You're not going to be wadded up with Barney, because it's much more convenient for you to make your mother happy by marrying me."

They hopped into the kitchen and rinsed their hands in the sink. Somehow he ended up loosening her end of the sheet, but Crystal gave a firm tug on it so she could stay covered. She glared at him. "Why did you kiss her?" she said suddenly. "Why did you kiss Kathryn if you were so in love with me?"

He put down the towel he'd been drying his hands with. "She was sad," he said simply.

She'd been pregnant and dumped. That would

make the most stalwart of hearts sad. "I wonder why she never told me. About the baby."

"Because she was frightened. She was ashamed. And when her boyfriend found out she was pregnant and broke up with her, she just…lost it."

It would be horrible. Crystal couldn't even imagine it. "I guess we could have ended up pregnant," she whispered. "We didn't use any protection that night."

He touched his nose to hers. "We were young. I may not like how our relationship ended, but your mother has a point. We were lucky in a strange sense."

"I think we might have been." She looked up into his eyes. "But I still don't want to feel all that emotion again. I don't want to fall like that. I'm at the age where safety nets look pretty appealing."

"Barney makes a large safety net. But I'm certain you could do with a taller, thinner one." He kissed the side of her neck. Shivers of delight ran through Crystal, and her heart began beating hard. She reached for the water and moved the lever to "on." Before Mitch could stop her, she took the vegetable sprayer and aimed at his end of the sheet, quickly soaking him.

He yelped, wrestling her for the sprayer. She squealed, slapping the water lever down and trying to hop out of the sheet before he could exact revenge.

But he was equally determined not to be outdone.

"Fifty-fifty," he said, catching her and dragging her to the floor. "Wet or dry."

"Fifty-fifty, with pneumonia or with good health," she panted as he covered her with his body. "But just until Mother is back to being her old self again, or six weeks, whichever comes first."

"Fifty-fifty, for better or worse," he agreed, sliding into her so that she gasped with pleasure. "But you have to promise that no matter what, we sleep in the same bed every night of the six weeks. I don't believe in going to bed angry. It's bad for the heart."

"Are you going to make me angry?" she asked, hanging on to his shoulders and wrapping her legs around his waist.

"Right now, I'm going to make you scream," he promised her. They moved against each other, panting and frenzied. "But in case anybody meddles in our convenient marriage, I want the chance to explain this time before you go flying off looking for that safety net."

"I don't know if this is such a good idea," Crystal said, her body about to splinter into shining fragments. "I'm afraid."

"Everybody's afraid of something," he said, his mouth tantalizingly hot against her ear. "You just have to let go, safety net or not."

She did, and went falling into the protection of his arms, her scream of fulfillment swallowed by his kiss.

"WE'RE GETTING MARRIED," Crystal told Bess and Martin and Elle as they sat around the hospital bed.

Bess stared at her and Mitch with great suspicion. "Where's your ring?" she demanded.

"That's wonderful!" Elle cried, jumping to her feet to hug Crystal and Mitch.

"Congratulations," said Uncle Martin, shaking Mitch's hand and giving his niece a peck on the cheek.

"Where's your ring?" Bess demanded again, her tone petulant. "Is this for real, or are you trying to pull the wool over these old eyes?"

"Oh, for heaven's sake," Crystal said, collapsing back into the chair. She had horrible butterflies just saying *we're getting married* and her mother wanted to squabble over insignificant details.

"I think your announcement has nothing to do with heaven or true love. I think you're doing this to make me happy," Bess said.

"Wasn't that the point?" Mitch asked. "You wanted us to get married. So we are."

"You wouldn't if I wasn't on my deathbed."

"You can't have it all, Bess," Mitch told her with a grin. "We're getting married. The circumstances are our own personal business. Mine and Crystal's." He reached to clasp Crystal's hand, and she relaxed greatly. It felt wonderful having him by her side.

That's the second time I've thought that.

She liked the security, she realized instantly.

Sharing her life with Mitch had been the only real dream she'd ever had. Fifty-fifty.

Her heart began to pull apart as Bess watched her closely. The problem was, she wasn't fooling anybody.

She was still in love with Mitch, and a marriage of convenience might be convenient, but it was going to hurt like hell when it ended. What they were really doing was entering into an arranged marriage, where they'd planned all the arrangements.

Unfortunately, she knew only too well that the best-laid plans sometimes went awry. She could name a few: Genie, Janet, Kathryn, herself.

The whole arrangement somehow felt dangerous to her equilibrium, and Crystal conceded she had never been one to laugh in the face of danger.

She didn't even feel like smiling.

BESS WAS WHEELED DOWN the hall toward the operating room. It was clear from her drawn face that she was not soothed in the least by the drugs they'd given her to relax.

"It's okay, Mama," Crystal whispered. "You're going to be fine."

"I'd be fine if Mitch was doing the procedure," Bess pronounced peevishly. "I had to put a total stranger in control of my health, and I'm quite certain nothing good can come of that, Mitch McStern. Even if you are marrying my daughter, which I have my doubts about until I see the marriage license, you should still be my surgeon."

"I can't, Bess," he said, patting her hand. "Forgive me on this one account. It's best that you allowed your physician to choose your surgeon. Dr. Halberstam has an excellent reputation."

"You're supposed to be the best heart-mender in the state." Her eyes were huge as she stared at him. "You haven't forgiven me for my confession about prom night. I knew it was a mistake to tell you, but I couldn't go to my grave with that on my conscience, especially since my secret has been keeping you two apart. You'd do the surgery if you didn't think I was a meddling, self-serving old dingbat."

Mitch shook his head with a smile and pulled back his hand. "Not true. And I'm not moving from the waiting area. Mine will be the first face you see when you awaken."

Slowly, she nodded. Barely. Not comforted at all. He could almost see her surrendering, running up the white flag of resignation. Mitch ground his teeth until her gurney was rolled into surgery.

Then he took a deep breath. Held in a shudder as best he could.

Everybody was afraid of something—and he was terrified of losing another patient he loved.

He could not have performed Bess's operation.

Chapter Ten

"I don't think that worked very well," Crystal said to Mitch as the waiting began. "Mother wasn't impressed with our engagement."

He surreptitiously wiped a fine sheen of sweat from the back of his neck and forced a weak grin. "We'll show her otherwise in two weeks when we marry."

"You're awfully pale." Crystal neared to look at him, her expression concerned. "Are you all right?"

"I'm fine. I think I'll get a drink of water."

He headed off, his chest tight. There wasn't any doubt in his mind that Bess would be fine. He hadn't even bothered to capitalize on Crystal's fears—though he could have—when he proposed to her, because he knew her mother was in the right hands. His conscience was clear on that score. He didn't have to be the hero-healer to Bess just to impress Crystal.

The very thought made his chest tighten again.

No, he'd advised his patient—no, not his patient but an old family friend—appropriately.

Now, getting Crystal into a wedding gown was something he wanted so much he thought he might die from the wanting, so he wasn't quite certain his conscience was as clear in that area. She was soft and sweet like she'd always been, and he had known utter ecstasy when they'd joined their bodies together. But he wasn't quite truthful about the convenience stuff. If that was what she needed to believe, then he'd give her plenty of space, but no way was he planning for this marriage to be simply a sham to make her family happy and give him some professional stability, no matter that he might have agreed to it in theory.

Couldn't he be just a tiny bit guilty on this matter? Having her this close to being his forever was a temptation he would never want to be cured from. He wanted her desperately—and he would love her from her toenails to her dainty ears.

Fortunately, she hadn't pushed him about performing the surgery on her mother. She probably didn't think he'd be reliable enough to show up. He'd let her down once before.

What she didn't know was that she was correct. He wasn't reliable and he wasn't the cardiac surgeon everyone thought he was.

He was too afraid.

It had happened when he'd least expected it. A girlfriend he'd dated in med school had developed unanticipated cardiac problems. She had come to see him, because of their past history somewhat, but mostly because he had developed a fine reputation in the cardiac field.

He had assured her she would be fine. It had felt good to comfort a woman to whom he'd once given a small piece of his heart. They had parted on comfortable, mutual terms, and now it felt comfortable and right to do what was really a rather routine medical procedure on an old friend of his.

To his utter horror, she had died the next day from infection. His mouth still dried out and his mind totally receded from thinking about it, but six months hadn't erased the bleak memory.

No matter that she had died as a result of infection and not his surgical skill. He had told her she'd be fine.

He'd been horribly wrong.

From that day forward, he vowed never again to operate on a patient he loved. The thought, the very consideration of trying again, sent him into a state of terror.

Crystal brought light and laughter into his life, and he desperately needed that. Now that he was so close to getting everything he had ever wanted back in his life, he wasn't about to do anything to screw it up.

Mitch decided Bess was right about the ring. Convenient or not, he was getting Crystal a ring that shouted Mine! Mine! Mine! Whether she wanted to think of him in nonconventional terms or not, he was firmly going to mark her with a significant token of his affection. They could work out the bumps of their agreement as the marriage progressed.

For that matter, he was going to plan the wedding. Crystal could handle the church details, but he'd let her down once in front of the whole town.

He would plan the reception—and it was going to be every bit as big and public as her birthday party. More talked-about than the prom.

This time, he would be there. He would prove to Crystal that she could count on him.

"MOTHER SHOULD BE COMING out anytime now." Crystal paced the waiting room. Mitch sat quietly in a corner. Martin and Elle pretended to read magazines.

Crystal took a deep breath and thought about drinking the first cup of coffee she'd ever drunk in her life. There was a coffeepot with some ink-black coffee nearby, but Crystal decided that trying to drink the unappealing liquid wouldn't take her mind off her mother's surgery and might very well give her a stomachache or caffeine-electrified nerves. She was frazzled enough.

"The nurse said she'd get us when Bess was coming around." Mitch got to his feet and put his hands on her shoulders. "I think we'd better celebrate by getting you an engagement ring."

Crystal felt herself smile. "I can't think about that right now."

"She's right, you know. We should make this

official, with an announcement in the town news-paper and everything. I'd like to do this right, even if it's a short-term thing.''

''Have you told your folks?''

He slapped his forehead. ''I completely forgot!''

''Maybe a marriage of convenience doesn't rate as much excitement as a regular one. We should keep the event as quiet as possible.''

He snorted. ''Getting you to an altar is a marquee event, trust me.''

She wound her arm into his, taking solace in his warmth. ''How come you never got married, Mitch?''

''Never felt like it. But I do now, despite having to beat Barney off to enter into this squirrely ar-rangement.''

She laughed. ''Maybe we should talk about our squirrely arrangement.''

He pulled her up against him. ''Okay. I'll feed the dogs, you bathe them. I'll feed the cats, you bathe them. I'll do the laundry, you vacuum. Con-venient enough?''

''Sounds like I'm getting a roomie instead of a husband.''

''Husband. Husband. I like the sound of that. Are you keeping your own name? I'm sure you are,'' he said woefully.

''I haven't thought that far,'' she said, smiling up at him. ''But the fifty-fifty definition of that would probably be yes, I am.''

"At least I get fifty percent of your bed." He sneaked a fast kiss.

"I'm going to have to tell the dogs they're sleeping on the floor from now on."

"Oh, boy. That will endear me to them." He grinned, not bothered by the dogs' looming disappointment at all. "By the way, I'm going to ask Barney to be my best man."

"You are?"

He nodded. "And Linc and Frankie to be ushers."

"Oh, joy." Crystal smiled. "I'm asking Janet to be my maid of honor. And Genie to be one of my bridesmaids. That leaves me with one less attendant than you."

"There's always Kathryn," he said with a wink until he saw the expression on Crystal's face. "Kidding! Kidding!" he cried, holding up an arm to ward off her sudden smack on his arm. "Well, she was once your best friend, you know."

"That was a long time ago." But strangely enough, she found herself giving his suggestion some real thought. So much had changed over the years. She and Kathryn had been close as sisters before that fateful night. "Wait a minute." She turned to face Mitch. "Whatever happened to her pregnancy?"

"Oh." He took his arm from Crystal's and scratched the back of his neck. "She miscarried. That's why she's so delighted about this pregnancy. She was really afraid she couldn't carry a pregnancy to term. I wish her husband would grow up and hang around some, the schmuck.''

''Oh, my goodness.'' Kathryn had even worse luck than Crystal. She felt sorry for her old friend. First a high school crush had walked out on her when she got pregnant, and now her husband was doing the same. ''So do you still keep up with her, Mitch?''

''Yeah. Her gynecologist is in the same medical complex as my office. So we have lunch when she comes to town.''

''I see.'' Mitch had had more than ample opportunity to date Kathryn over the years and hadn't. She had let a friendship get away from her for nothing. ''How did you end up taking her to the prom, anyway?''

''She came to my house upset, all dressed up, about twenty minutes before I was to pick you up. I guess she'd been talking to your mother and Bess suggested she ask me to go. All I ever knew was that you weren't feeling well, and that you wanted me to go with Kathryn to the prom. I thought nothing of it since she was upset about being dumped, and you two were best friends. She said you'd gone to bed. Next thing I knew you weren't speaking to me.'' He caught her hand in his. ''I suppose your mother didn't want us together at all.''

''All these years I've been angry with you, and I should have been angry with my mother. But I can't be angry with her, because she's convinced her guilty secret has made her ill.'' Crystal gazed at him, remembering how she had decided never to speak to Mitch again when she learned he'd gone to the prom with Kathryn. She'd been convinced something had happened to him. Then her mother had called—pretended to call?—Mitch's house and broken the news. "Of course, that still doesn't explain the kiss. I know you said she was sad, but for some reason, I feel somehow jealous."

He looked perplexed for a moment, then leaned over and gave her a fast peck next to the lips.

"What was that?"

"The same kiss I gave Kathryn."

"That was it?" She could hardly believe he was telling her the truth.

He shrugged. "Crystal, you and I had just made love the night before. I wasn't exactly thinking about making out with anyone else."

"I want to believe you," she murmured.

"You have to believe in your husband," he said. "That's in the marriage vows, isn't it?"

"Not if you're Kathryn." Crystal felt depressed for her old friend. She thought about the dog bowl Kathryn had painted for her birthday gift. "I'll ask her to be in the wedding. She may not be feeling up to such excitement, but I can ask. She can hold my hand if you don't show up for our wedding."

Mitch gave her a squeeze. "I'm going to be there. Count on it. Nothing could keep me from seeing you in a wedding gown."

"You can visit your mom for a few moments,"

the nurse called into the waiting room. "She did just fine. And she's asking for you."

"Oh!" Crystal hurried into the hallway and then the recovery room, with Mitch following close behind. "Mother," she said softly as she neared the temporary hospital bed. "How are you feeling?"

"I think I feel wonderful as far as the body goes. But I had a nightmare that you and Mitch were just pretending to get married so I wouldn't have negative vibes during surgery." She peered at both of them from squinty eyes. "You are getting married, aren't you?"

"In two weeks," Mitch assured her. "And then we're taking a honeymoon cruise to the Bahamas a week after that."

"We are?" Crystal whirled to face him.

"Yes. We'd leave right after the wedding, but I have some upcoming…um, business I can't get away from, and I thought you'd probably need a little more time to find someone to work in your shop. Is that all right?"

"Martin and Elle and I can handle the shop just fine," Bess said petulantly. "We are experts in wedding dreams."

He smiled at Crystal as he realized she hesitated. "Being on a ship in the middle of the ocean ought to convince you that I mean to stay by your side, Crystal Jennings."

"Handcuffs would be more convincing," she stated with a wry smile for her mother's benefit.

"Who wants handcuffs?" Uncle Martin asked as

he and Aunt Elle came to join them. "Bess? They threatening to handcuff you to keep you in bed?"

"No." Bess closed her eyes with a weary smile. "After all these years, Mitch and Crystal have decided to get handcuffed."

"I think she's tired," Crystal said to Mitch.

"Still a little dopey," he agreed. "Let's go pick out our handcuffs while she sleeps it off."

"The purpose of a convenient marriage is to not feel handcuffed," Crystal said.

"You're going to like wearing my handcuffs," he assured her.

They left, smiling at each other.

Elle stared at her brother. "I'm confused. Who's wearing handcuffs?"

Martin shook his head. "Ever since Sister said she'd been behind Mitch not showing up the night of the prom, I've tried to ignore everything as it transpires."

"I wish Sister was the only one at fault," Elle said, clasping her hands together as she stared down at her sleeping sister. "I told Mitch to go down to the wedding shop to see Crystal. I didn't exactly reel him in by accident."

"That wasn't a coincidence?"

"It was not," Elle said on a pained gasp. "He had called the house to inquire after her. I seized the chance to fix up our girl. We agreed to meet at Crystal's shop, and Mitch was waiting for me to give him the signal to come inside after I'd softened Crystal up to see him for the first time since they'd broken up. I never got around to it before Sister issued her challenge. So, I reached out the door and jerked him inside.''

"You are a sly one," he said admiringly. "To make it seem so coincidental."

"Don't tell Crystal. Matters are going so well, even if she is handcuffing him to her, or vice versa!''

He shook his head. "I won't say a word. I'm a great believer in leaving all family skeletons firmly locked away.''

Elle let out a great sigh. "Once upon a time, I thought that, too. But now that I've told someone I meddled, I feel ever so much better.''

Martin shook his head. "I have no confession I care to make at this time. And I'm feeling just fine!''

THE HANDCUFF MITCH WANTED to put on Crystal was a two carat diamond, perfectly oval-shaped.

"It's very extravagant for a marriage of convenience, don't you think?" she asked.

"Is there a guide we could consult? I have no idea what is considered proper in our situation," he said, his gaze teasing.

"I don't think there is a guide," she said, sniffing. "I'm only suggesting that you don't have to spend so much on something that isn't permanent."

"Wait. This is permanent."

She was startled. "It is?"

"Yes. All I thought I was agreeing to was to go

out with my friends whenever I wanted to, like Barney. And you're agreeing to do your own thing, whatever that is. But it's permanent.''

She digested that, her pulse suddenly erratic.

''So it's convenient, but it's also forever in my mind. It's the only way to have a marriage, Crystal. Don't you like the ring?''

''It's lovely.'' Somehow the new heaviness on her hand was comforting and gave her a welcome sense of security she desperately wanted. ''Try one on. You'll probably like it.''

He picked up a gold band.

''It's not as extravagant as mine. Don't you want a band with diamonds or something?''

''I'm not a flashy guy. This works fine.''

She frowned. ''Maybe mine is too flashy.''

''I want everyone within a mile to know you're conveniently married.''

A thrill tightened her stomach. ''That's putting a twist on the term, I suppose.''

''I thought so. Let's go show Bess so she can recover in peace.''

''She won't. As soon as she sees this ring, she's going to wear out the phone company calling all her friends.''

He kissed her thoroughly. ''We'll insist she rest often.''

''Thank you, Mitch. Not just for the ring, but…for forgiving my family and taking such steps to reassure my mother.''

''I'm not marrying you to reassure your mother.

It may have started out that way, but that's not the way I feel at all about you. I'm starting to like this convenience thing.''

She closed her eyes, not ready to hear him express deeper feelings. He didn't say he loved her, and she finally breathed a sigh of relief. Opening her eyes, she said, "I'm not marrying you to reassure my mother, either."

"I'm marrying you to keep you from Barney's clutches."

She nodded. "That's good enough for me."

BESS RECOVERED QUICKLY, the scent of wedding triumph speeding her health as she slowly rehabilitated in her home. "I can't wait! I can't wait! I must see your gown!" she insisted to Crystal.

"Absolutely not. Not even my husband can see the bridal gown." Crystal was adamant on this point.

"All that talk of handcuffs makes me nervous. Promise me you're not going to strut down the aisle in something Genie would wear," she said.

"Just wait and see." Crystal held in a shiver of anticipation. Everything was going better than she could have hoped. Mitch slept with her every night, claiming his right to his fifty percent of her bed. The dogs had adjusted nicely; the cats welcomed an extra hand to scratch them under their chins. Kathryn had readily agreed to be in her wedding, although Crystal had truly dreaded talking to her, fearing her old friend wouldn't say yes. But Kathryn had—with great enthusiasm and gratitude at leaving the past behind.

Crystal couldn't have been happier until the nerves set in.

"Bridal nerves are common," Bess told her.

"Every bride has them," Elle counseled.

"A little bit of nerves is good," Martin comforted. "Keeps you on your toes."

Crystal didn't want to say that her nerves had spread to throwing up in the night.

"Maybe you're pregnant," Mitch suggested.

"Shut up," Crystal said on a groan as he ran a cool cloth over her forehead. "That would not be my idea of bedside humor."

"I wasn't exactly trying to be funny, but never mind."

She groaned when Kathryn, Genie and Janet sat in her salon that afternoon.

"I didn't get nerves until after my wedding, when I realized Tom was a jerk," Kathryn said. "Then I had nerves."

"I didn't get nerves, but then, I married Linc so fast I didn't have time to," Genie said happily. "But I didn't get them after the fact, either. I love him so much."

Janet took a deep breath. "You know, Crystal, even though Mitch is my brother, I would feel guilty if I didn't remind you that we had a similar conversation about nerves when I was engaged. It resulted in my breaking off the engagement."

Crystal winced. "Don't remind me."

"Maybe you should give your advice some consideration," Janet said gently. "Genie and I want you to be happy, no matter what you decide. But you wouldn't be suffering so if everything was copacetic."

"Fine bridal consultant I am to need advice from my attendants," Crystal grumbled. "I don't know what's wrong with me."

"Maybe you should listen to your fiancé the doctor and give the home pregnancy test a whirl," Kathryn suggested.

"Ugh!" She shot Kathryn's burgeoning stomach a frightened glance. "It's nerves, nothing more."

"Then you better settle them, Crystal." Kathryn moved to a more comfortable position on the large sofa. "You're planning the biggest day of your life—well, until you decide to have children. You want it to be everything you ever dreamed of. Everything you ever did for any other bride."

"She's right, Crystal," Genie agreed. "I loved what you did for me."

"It was just shoes and a dress," Crystal said glumly. "That's all I've ever given any bride, I suppose."

"Not Janet or me," Genie said. "You gave us incentive to be ourselves."

Crystal snapped her fingers. "Maybe that's the problem! I've got good-girl blues. Every night Mitch and I sleep together and I love having him with me. But somewhere in the night, my mind reminds me that we're putting the cart before the horse by making love so much. So I throw up.''

"Nope," Kathryn disagreed. "Making love is a calming thing. It should be done as often as possible if you love your man. You wouldn't feel guilty about that."

She did. She felt guilty for making love with Mitch and enjoying it so much when she wasn't ready to give him her whole heart. Was she satisfied with the agreement they'd struck?

"I wish I'd made love with Tom more before we got married," Kathryn said softly. "Because of my…um, situation in high school, I felt like I should wait until after I got married before I engaged in sexual relations. But that really didn't work, either," she said, her tone sad. "My over-eager ovaries immediately reacted to lovemaking with a pregnancy, and my husband walked out soon after saying we weren't as compatible in bed as he thought we'd be. He travels a lot now, and I know it's to avoid my…um, our marriage. So I'd say make love all you can, particularly if you're enjoying it. That would be my advice."

"I am so sorry, Kathryn! I had no idea." Crystal went to the sofa to hug her friend.

Janet and Genie patted Kathryn's hands and shoulders.

Kathryn laughed, full and throaty, and resolutely pushed their hands away. "I'm not looking for sympathy today, although I thank you for your concern. I just want you to know that you're probably not suffering from good-girl blues, Crystal.''

''Probably not.'' But she wished it was as simple as sexual conscience. The real problem glimmered into focus as she thought through Kathryn's story.

She and Mitch lay in bed together every night. They made love. They talked about general things. They co-planned some of their honeymoon travel details.

They did not talk about Mitch, she suddenly realized. Any time she had asked him about his practice or his life before they had met each other again, Mitch kissed her. Or he tickled her. Or he made love to her.

But he never, ever talked about his life. All she knew was that he seemed to be taking a break from practicing medicine.

Her stomach clenched tight as she fought a wave of nausea. In ten days she was marrying a man she hadn't known in a long time—and the years in between the times they'd dated were a blank.

For a woman who wanted a safety net, she was jumping without one.

''What you need,'' Genie said cheerfully, ''is your bridesmaids to take your place.''

''What?'' Crystal wasn't sure where that fit in.

''You need to be the customer, and we will be the bridal consultants!'' A grin lit her elfin features.

Crystal held back a groan. ''I don't know—''

''You need motivation! Once you get started with wedding preparations, you'll forget all about your nerves. You just need help!'' Genie jumped to her feet. ''There are three of us to take little ol' you in hand. We'll each choose a gown we think you'd be scrumptious in, and you can select one of our ensembles!''

''Just think,'' Kathryn said dryly, ''we have a variety of taste, Crystal. This should be fun.''

''Being a victim is never fun.'' But she sat back against the sofa, too frozen by her realization to refuse their offer. ''I could probably use a kick start.''

''Oh, it's much too difficult to do everything for yourself!'' Janet airily stated. ''If you were a doctor, you wouldn't necessarily heal yourself, would you?''

Physician heal thyself doesn't work with me, Mitch had said.

Chills swept her. ''I don't think so.''

''Well, then. Let's go, girls.'' Janet went off, the other women following her.

Crystal sighed, making herself relax. She picked up the phone next to the sofa and dialed Mitch's parents' house.

''Hello?''

His voice on the line after two rings startled Crystal. ''It's Crystal, Mitch.''

''Hi! I'm on the other line with the caterers. Do you want to hold or what?''

''I want to talk to you. When you have time.''

''I'm going to have all night,'' he said, his tone suggestive.

She closed her eyes. "Mitch, something just occurred to me."

"Can it wait until after I tell the caterers what kind of libations we want at the wedding?"

"Mitch, you haven't been going to Dallas," she said on a rush, "and all of a sudden, I realized you don't seem to be working. Or not very much. Not that I'm familiar with the hours a cardiac surgeon works, but—"

"Let's talk about this tonight, okay? I've got to get back to the caterers. But I'll bring something over for dinner, if you think you'll be hungry. How are you feeling?"

Sick. She wanted to say, *I feel nervous and tense and in doubt.*

Genie came into the salon with her choice of wedding attire and Crystal swallowed. "I feel...like I'm falling."

"I've fallen for you, too, babe. Talk to you later."

She hung up, eyeing Genie and the short minidress sparkling at her. "Um—"

"Short and white, clean and bright!" Genie chirped. "Modern fairy-bride attire."

"I'm not Tinkerbell, though." Crystal told herself to give her bridal consultant's suggestion a fair consideration.

"But you've got great legs. You should lose those long skirts you wear and show your groom a little skin."

"You think standing at the altar is the time to

make a fashion change?'' If she made a major change in her approach to clothing on her wedding day, she might feel self-conscious.

"You looked great in that red dress you wore at your party, and that was very short."

"Aunt Elle picked that out for me." Crystal would never have chosen anything like that, always wishing to appear professional and calm.

"And I thought you looked sensational. So did Mitch." Genie grinned at her. "Try it. You might like it."

Janet came out into the salon, holding a long, lavish ecru gown encrusted with seed pearls and sequins. The neckline was sweetheart and the sleeves were cap-style.

"That one is lovely," Crystal said reluctantly. "Very elegant. Very romantic."

"You'd look like a princess," Janet said, "and every woman should feel like a princess on her wedding day."

Crystal folded her lips. "I'm sure you have a point—'' The trouble was, she felt more like a fraud than a princess. But she resolved to try the dress on.

Kathryn came in with nothing in her hands. Crystal raised her eyebrows.

"I couldn't find anything. Nothing in here seems to jive with who you are," she said apologetically. "I'm sorry, Crystal."

Relieved, Crystal jumped to her feet. "That's

what's bothering me! I don't need a wedding gown at all! I need to elope!''

"Why?" Kathryn frowned at her. "Just because I can't find the real you in lace-over-satin? Give me a chance. You've got catalogs galore, and a trip into Dallas wouldn't be amiss."

But Crystal shook her head, her stomach easing. "I think I'm not a big-wedding kind of girl. A basic elopement would suit me fine."

"I think your mom would be terribly disappointed," Kathryn said. "Not to mention Mitch."

Crystal studied the glittering diamond on her hand for a moment before saying, "I know." Mitch wanted a big wedding to help her erase her worries about him being a man she could count on.

But after all these years, she didn't know him the way she once had—and she had a bad feeling their marriage of convenience wasn't quite fifty-fifty in honesty. "This is such a bad idea," she said in a whisper none of her friends heard as they planned her dream wedding.

The door opened, and Kathryn's husband, Tom, surprised everyone by walking in the door. He saw his heavily pregnant wife with the long skirt of satin and sparkles Janet had selected for Crystal, and went ecru himself. "Your mother told me you were here. I need to talk to you, Kathryn."

The wondrous fabric fell from Kathryn's fingers. "I didn't know you were back in town, Tom."

He glanced at Crystal and Janet and Genie with

some unease. "I'm only in for the afternoon. Actually, I just came here to tell you...to tell you—"

"Tell me what?"

Crystal watched hope flare in Kathryn's eyes. She waited breathlessly for Tom to finish. Maybe there were happy endings, maybe her friend would have a chance for a happy marriage—

"I'm getting married as soon as our divorce is final," he stated, before turning and walking back out the door.

Chapter Eleven

"It was horrible!" Crystal told Mitch as they ate a dinner of pizza and beer. The dogs sat outside the kitchen window dolefully watching them; the cats ignored them. Crystal had set her painted teacup on the table but found herself unable to use it. Kathryn had been shattered by her husband's announcement, and Crystal was heartbroken for her.

She was also more worried than ever about marrying Mitch, conveniently or otherwise.

"He just walked out. Just left her standing there." Crystal could completely relate to the suffering and emptiness of being dumped. "I don't think I can eat any more." She pushed herself away from the table and put her plate in the sink.

"You've got to eat sometime," Mitch said. "As a doctor, I advise you against forgoing this pizza. It's pretty good."

"You don't seem sorry for Kathryn at all," Crystal said. "I know you're one of the few people she's ever counted on."

He sighed. "Crystal, she'll come to me when

she's ready to talk. I'm sure right now she's trying to be respectful of our relationship.''

''You mean that she won't come to you because of me?'' Crystal couldn't bear that.

''Well, obviously, it's a bad situation for her, but she's known for a while that Tom was a slime.''

''She's pregnant!''

''And she's tough. She'll make it through this. She's never been a fainting flower of a female.''

Crystal turned around to face him. ''Are you suggesting I'm fainthearted?''

''No. You just have different approaches to men.''

''I don't have any approach to men!'' Crystal glared at him.

''That's my point. She'll find another man. She won't hide from her pain. And no, I'm not taking a shot at you.''

Crystal crossed her arms. ''Are you speaking from experience, then? Are you hiding something from me?''

He put his pizza down, clearly unhappy with her observation. Indecision folded his finely shaped lips and creased a line between his eyes. He set his jaw squarely in irritation.

She seated herself at the table again and clasped his hands over the plates. ''Mitch, maybe it's time we talk and get everything out in the open. Everything. We can do it before, or we can do it after, but it looks to me like doing it before is better than saving it all for later.''

"I'd like to take that as a sexual innuendo—"

She shook her head and skipped the smile.

He sighed. "I'm being sued for negligence."

The single sentence shocked Crystal.

"And to be perfectly honest, I don't think I want to practice medicine anymore," he said. "And that's the confession I've been hiding, Crystal."

To SAY THAT HE HADN'T wanted to tell her his secret was an understatement. Being so close to having her forever, he wanted to present himself in the very best light possible. Yet, like Bess, keeping his secret inside him hadn't felt right.

Once upon a time, he and Crystal had shared everything. That was the way he remembered her, as his best friend, as the girl he loved to talk to and be with and kiss for hours.

He'd known he was being selfish—but God help him, he in no way intended to have a sham marriage. And that was something else they needed to get straight. "Confession's painful," he said tiredly. "I'd rather get a shot."

"What do you mean you're being sued? You weren't going to tell me?"

His chest rose and fell with a regretful sigh. "We weren't going to use the same funds or have the same bank account, as I recall, so there was no danger of your money being affected—"

Crystal stood up. "Is there a reason you haven't told me this?"

"It's not something I relish." He also stood but

made no move toward her. "In fact, the only way I've been able to even forget it long enough to be able to sleep is…when I'm with you at night."

CRYSTAL TRIED TO PUT a brave face on what Mitch had told her, but she still felt as if she'd been left standing at the prom without a date. How could he not have told her?

On the other hand, maybe it didn't change what they'd agreed to, she argued with herself.

Her mother had called it right. She'd never gotten over him, so she'd hidden away, shielding her broken heart.

Okay, so their marriage of convenience would be missing some vital ingredients, Crystal thought later as they made love in her bed, surrounded by sleeping pets on the floor, under the bed and along the bookshelves. But she and Mitch were happiest in each other's arms, and that had to be as good a place to start as any.

They both slept through the night without waking.

"I HAVE A NEW LEASE on life," Bess told Crystal when she visited her mother the next day.

"I'm feeling pretty repaired myself."

"Have you picked out a gown?" Bess beamed. "I want to hear every detail. I want to hear about the lace, the length, and how the sequins are going to sparkle as much as that diamond Mitch gave you."

Elle and Martin smiled approvingly. Crystal felt a small clutch of dismay but forced it back. "I haven't quite picked one out yet—"

"Oh, Crystal," her mother said sorrowfully.

"But I've narrowed it down to a few choices!" she quickly inserted.

"And you owning a bridal salon, too," Bess said ruefully. "Why, you're just trying to placate me. I know you too well, Crystal Star Jennings. Once you make up your mind, you're fast as lightning. What girl doesn't jump to pick out her wedding gown?" She folded her lips. "I don't need to be a mind reader to know that as soon as the doctor proclaims me fit, you two will call off this supposed engagement."

"We're not calling anything off," Crystal insisted.

"Good, because I put an announcement in the *Lover's Valley Herald*." Bess held out the paper so that Crystal could take it.

She did, reluctantly, her eyes stretched with disbelief and a fresh sense of panic. "Mother! I wasn't planning to invite the entire town to the wedding!"

Her three family members stared at her in dismay.

"Mitch said it was just what he wanted," Elle said plaintively. "He did say he wanted to have a very public affair. He suggested the gym, in fact. I believe he said that, in order to erase old ghosts, the two of you needed to return to the scene of the original disappointment. Meaning the prom night that never was.''

Crystal felt tremors begin to shake her stomach. ''I'm not certain I'm ready for such a big step.'' How could she allow the whole town to witness her humiliation if —

It's not like last time, she told herself sternly. *Mitch wants to marry me.* And church or gym, it didn't matter. The high school gym was actually the more practical choice since it was larger. But she got goose bumps thinking about returning there for a sentimental occasion. She'd spent hours helping decorate it for prom night.

''Is that even a diamond, or just cubic zirconia to fob me off?'' Bess wanted to know. ''Something you can simply toss in the trash when this charade is over?''

''I can't believe I'm hearing this,'' Crystal said on a groan. ''When did you become so suspicious-minded?''

''Since you've avoided the altar for years.'' Bess shook her head. ''My only child, my daughter, the light of my life. An avowed bachelorette, a cello-phane-wrapped leftover of her own making. I just simply do not comprehend the problem. If you weren't such a beautiful, sweet girl maybe I could understand, but my daughter deserves the best man in the state of Texas.'' She crossed her arms. ''And I don't think I'm tooting my own horn too much to say that I did a damn fine job raising you to be such a special woman. It isn't right for you to leave your charms in a box in a dark closet where they can't be shared with people who have so much less.''

Crystal gritted her teeth, positive she felt hives breaking out along her back. "Mom, in two days, I will be a bride. Even if it kills me. You'll just have to wait until the happy day for proof. Other than that, I wish you'd keep your dire proclamations to yourself. Please. You'll get your chance to be a beaming mother of the bride, I promise.''

"If you're happy, I'm happy," Bess said primly. "I just want you to be happy.''

"I'm not as happy as I am confused!" Crystal gathered up her purse. "I'm feeling distinctly disoriented after having this conversation.''

"Mitch can probably prescribe something for you," Bess said brightly. "Kissing him three times a day, maybe?''

"He's not my physician," Crystal said sternly. She wouldn't say that right now he was no one's physician. Not even his own.

But she had kind of liked learning that he found relief from his pain by being with her.

THE RINGING OF THE PHONE in the middle of the night sent both Mitch and Crystal and the dogs upright with surprise.

"Who could be calling at this hour?" Crystal gasped. She jerked the phone up and turned it on. "Hello? Mrs. McStern?''

She listened for a moment. "Oh, my goodness!

Oh, no! Of course. Um, yes. I'll…tell him right now. He'll be there as soon as possible.''

She switched off the phone and turned on a light to face Mitch. ''Kathryn's been in a horrible car crash! There's something wrong with her heart or the baby's heart or something. I didn't get all the details from your mom. But you're needed at the hospital right away. Kathryn is asking for you. She doesn't want anyone else performing the surgery.''

His eyes went wide under his sexily rumpled hair. She saw the muscles in his chest tense.

This was no time for him to dwell on the past. She hopped out of bed. ''Get up, Mitch, damn it! Put these clothes on.''

She swept him a pair of jeans and her nerveless fingers grabbed the Just Do It T-shirt he wore when he lounged in front of the TV with her at night. ''Hurry, damn it!''

When he didn't move, she jammed the T-shirt over his head and dragged him from the bed to his feet. ''Mitch, snap out of it! This is an emergency. You better than anyone know how much Kathryn wants that baby.'' She hopped up on the bed so that she was directly in his face. When he didn't look at her, she shook him. ''Listen to me. I know you're scared. You have reason to be. But she's asking for you. You. The finest cardiac surgeon around. So get going and do the job. Because if you don't and something happens to her or the baby—'' She took a deep breath. ''Mitch, I don't think you'd ever forgive yourself if you let something happen to her.

And frankly, we'll all be living in the past forever.'' She pulled his head to hers so that she could give him a fast kiss on the lips. Then she looked into his eyes, forcing him to connect with her. "I don't want that. Do you?"

"I'm going," he said hoarsely through lips that barely moved.

"Excellent." Crystal hopped off the bed and grabbed up a pair of jeans for herself and a T-shirt that had way too much dog hair clinging to it as she ran for her keys. "So am I. I'll drive."

Chapter Twelve

Mitch wasn't going to do the surgery. He could calm Katherine down and get his buddy Halberstam in to do the actual procedure. He would be backup instead.

He called Ron Halberstam on his cell phone and made arrangements to meet him at the hospital. Crystal listened while she drove without saying a word. Disapproval might be lingering on the air but he couldn't worry about that. She simply did not understand how frozen he was. This was not the time for him to pick up the scalpel again.

At the hospital, he and Crystal ran to Kathryn. To his surprise, there were no nurses scurrying to prep her for surgery.

Instead, she was being instructed to push by a birthing nurse.

"Kathryn," he said, going to take her hand. Crystal was less reserved, hurrying to hug her friend.

"What is her condition?" he asked the nurse. "I thought there was some suspected cardiac trauma."

"They weren't certain when they called you," the nurse answered. "I believe they wanted you on hand in case the baby was in distress."

"Should she be having a section?" Mitch noticed that Kathryn seemed calm and confident, if somewhat disheveled from the accident. A large bruise was beginning to darken her upper arm, so he inspected that and began to examine her other arm and neck. "Is there indication of fetal distress?"

"No. Although we weren't positive when she was brought in. Mrs. Vincent was quite upset about her pregnancy, and the accident apparently caused her to begin labor. As for the section, she has opted to try to deliver vaginally until we advise her that the baby is at risk."

Obviously his mother had overstated Kathryn's condition when she phoned Crystal's house, but his mother would have panicked and the medical jargon would have upset her, not the least because it was someone she knew.

"Mitch," Kathryn said, after the labor pain had eased. "I knew you would come."

"Of course." Well, only after Crystal kicked his butt into gear. Now he was glad she'd delivered him up from his paralyzing memories. It had felt so bad to find his feet unable to move, his mouth unable to speak.

He glanced at Crystal as she held Kathryn's hand. *Later I'll tell her how much she means to me. I'll tell her how much I need her.*

Kathryn began panting again. She made a brave effort not to cry out. He watched the contraction pass across the monitor, saw it peak and then subside. His adrenaline had felt that way tonight. Frightening peak, draining valley.

"And, Crystal," Kathryn said when she finally could. "After everything, you really are my best friend."

"Of course! A prom night is nothing compared to a baby being born, is it?"

He was proud of Crystal. Only he knew how petrified she was of commitment, of putting her trust in another person. That she viewed the altar with the same misgivings she would view a hangman's gallows.

"Kathryn, just relax and breathe," Crystal told her. "You're doing fine, and soon you're going to be a mother."

She had a hideous bruise on her face. Another inch over and it could have been her temple. Mitch didn't even want to think about that. "Besides the labor, how are you feeling?"

"Sore. Angry. And a bit silly for taking a turn as fast as I did." Kathryn accepted an ice chip from Crystal and shook her head. "I was so upset about...Tom and everything that I was driving recklessly. I'm lucky I only hurt myself. I could have injured my baby, or someone else." A tear rolled down her face. "I don't think I could live with myself if I hit some innocent driver. Or family.'' Another contraction hit her, and she concentrated on the pain.

Mitch turned away, wrestling with his demons. He knew just what Kathryn meant. He was a doctor. He was supposed to heal, not harm.

TEN MINUTES LATER, Ron Halberstam strode into Kathryn's room. He was tall, handsome, confident, with burnished skin. Crystal was riveted by the air of command the man carried with him.

''Mitch,'' he said.

''Ron. This is my fiancée, Crystal, and this is the patient, Kathryn Vincent.''

''You don't look like a cardiac patient,'' Ron said, moving to Kathryn's bedside.

Crystal released Kathryn's hand and crossed to the other side of the room so that Ron could examine Kathryn's chart and speak to her.

''My hand is sore!'' Crystal whispered to Mitch. ''I can't imagine what I'd be feeling like if I'd had a car wreck and then went into labor! In fact, labor doesn't look all that inviting. I don't think I'll try it.''

''Never?''

She wrinkled her nose. ''I know that there's a wonderful prize to be had at the end of the race, but I never was good at track. I'll just stick to my pooches and felines.''

''I'd stay with you every second,'' he whispered against her ear. ''I'd never leave your side.''

''Not a reassuring thought. I'm pretty sure I

wouldn't want you around. I don't think I'd handle being a patient as well as Kathryn." She sighed and turned into his shoulder. "I can tell Kathryn is upset about Tom. I can't blame her. You think he'd at least be here for the sake of his child!"

Barney Fearing walked into the room. "Did I miss the party?" he asked.

"Barney!" Kathryn struggled to sit up and run a hand through her mussed hair. "What are you doing here?"

"Tom called me. He's in San Francisco, but apparently the hospital somehow got a message to him that you'd had an accident. He asked if I'd come by and check on you."

He set an enormous vase with twenty-four pink roses on the windowsill and came over to kiss her cheek.

"What a louse Tom is," Crystal muttered under her breath. "I'd like to give him a piece of my mind!"

"You just let them handle their own situation," Mitch advised. "Tom may have been held up somehow and couldn't get away. It's nice that he asked Barney to come by."

Crystal eyed him impatiently. "She needs her husband with her right now, not a bunch of friends."

"I don't know," Mitch said thoughtfully. "Barney was probably the right person for Tom to call on."

Crystal turned as Ron came over to talk to Mitch.

"She's stable," Ron commented.

"Sorry about the urgency," Mitch said sheepishly. "I jumped the gun. Mom called Crystal's with the message that Kathryn had been brought in and that there was some cardiac trauma. I should have examined her before I called you from your bed."

"Absolutely not. I'm glad to be here." The two men shook hands again. Crystal tried not to gawk at the big man. Her best estimate was that somehow he had the physique of Sylvester Stallone, with the coloring and handsome looks of Ricky Martin. She couldn't imagine a man so big operating on something so small as a heart. His hands were so large she felt certain he could hold a grapefruit in his palm the way she might hold a Ping-Pong ball.

Janet and Genie walked into the hallway outside Kathryn's room. Upon seeing Crystal and Mitch, they quietly came inside the room. Total relief was etched upon their faces as they saw Kathryn was fine. Then Mitch introduced Ron to his sisters, and Crystal watched the big man's eyes begin to glow as he assessed Janet.

"Are you all right, Crystal?" Mitch asked.

"Yes. I'm just admiring—I mean, I'm just amazed by everything that has happened tonight. If you'll excuse me, everybody," she said, hurrying back over to Kathryn's bedside before she made an utter fool of herself. "Barney! You're kind to rush right over here," she whispered across Kathryn's stomach to where he sat opposite her.

"I'm glad to do it," he said, his grin toothy as ever. "I've never seen a baby being born. Jes' foals and other livestock on the farm. This is special."

Crystal smiled at Barney. They both allowed Kathryn to squeeze their hands as she panted through another contraction.

Barney reached up to put a cool cloth against her forehead and feed her an ice chip. "Relax," he told her. "You're doing fine."

"Are you sure you don't mind being here?" Kathryn gasped.

"Naw. It's jes' like a football game. Pretty lady, you just set up for the pass and I'll catch that little pigskin when you're good and ready. I've never dropped one yet."

Kathryn smiled luminously, and Barney grinned back at her, and Crystal wondered why life was so mixed-up sometimes.

MITCH WAS GLAD Barney showed up. For some reason, the big man had a calming effect on Kathryn. Mitch's hands felt shaky. Not that they trembled, but the surgeon's steel nerves he had once possessed appeared to be gone.

He was grateful for Crystal. He was also somewhat ashamed. He shouldn't have had to be dragged—but once he'd gotten to the hospital and discovered Kathryn was going to be fine, he found himself enjoying the birth process.

And strangely, he found himself wondering how the birth process would be with Crystal. They had not agreed to have children—but as a baby's cry sounded in the room, he knew he would love to share a moment such as this with her.

This was not in their marriage of convenience agreement, though. He cleared his throat, watching Barney snuggle the now-cleaned and securely wrapped infant girl to his chest. Kathryn, tired and wan but extremely proud, stared up from the bed, her eyes large and definitely on Barney. If he had been an outsider looking in, he would have thought that Barney was the father of this infant, a very proud father.

He tugged Crystal close to him. She glanced up at him, startled, but made no move to leave his side. The tears in her eyes spoke volumes about her feeling about the new life they had witnessed being born.

"That was amazing," she said.

"Yeah, I thought so, too."

They didn't say anything for a few minutes.

"Maybe we should add an amendment to our agreement," he suggested.

She held his gaze, her eyes huge and questioning.

"I think you'd be a great mother."

"Do you?" she asked. There was a tremor in her voice. "I was just thinking you'd make a wonderful father."

They watched as Barney and Kathryn stared down at the baby now held by its mother.

"Thank you for being here for Kathryn," Crystal said.

Shock filled him, washing the shame away. "I wasn't there for her."

"You were. You're right here. One of the finest doctors in the country. And you had Dr. Halberstam in the room. How many women can say that they have a staff of highly qualified physicians assisting their labor nurse and delivering doctor?"

When she put it that way, he began to realize how multi-faceted Crystal was. She saw even his negative attributes through a positive prism. Pride filled an empty space in his chest. "Your mother's right about you," he finally said.

"Oh, gosh, whatever it is, please don't listen to my mother," Crystal said on a groan. "You know she has my best interests at heart, which is scary. And she's not above shaping things to suit her."

He looked at her gleaming blond hair, much like fine gold silk. Her eyes glimmered, reminding him of soft velvet one might showcase valuable diamonds upon. Skin silky as heavenly clouds lay just under his fingertips as he clasped her hand in his.

Oh, Bess was right. Crystal Star was a wonderful woman, heaven-sent. He desperately wanted to believe she could be his, forever.

THAT NIGHT WAS THE DREADED meeting with the minister for premarital counseling. Crystal had known the minister all her life, but she was still anxious about it. How could she talk about love and making a marriage work when both she and Mitch had entered into their agreement as if it were a business partnership? She felt dishonest.

But Pastor Richardson seemed not to notice her hesitation as he welcomed them both into his office.

"Come in, come in," he told them. "This is one wedding I'm very much looking forward to!"

He shook Mitch's hand and gave Crystal a hug. "Two of my favorite people. I wondered if you would ever manage to get together. The Lord works in mysterious ways, doesn't He?"

Crystal felt the back of her neck begin to itch. "Yes," she whispered. Less divine intervention and more Bess intervention was the case. Mitch squeezed her hand. She sensed him trying to calm her, so Crystal smiled and forgot about how they'd gotten together.

"So tonight we're going to talk about loving each other and nurturing each other in a committed relationship, right?" He leaned forward and put his spectacles on, which only served to make his merry blue eyes seem more intense as he looked at Crystal. "Are you okay, Crystal? There's nothing to be apprehensive about."

"I'm fine," she replied. But even to her the answer didn't sound firm.

He smiled at her reassuringly. "You seem a trifle un-Crystal, perhaps, but I promise you, this is the good part. Talking about growing a loving relationship is a very rewarding experience."

She swallowed. She glanced at Mitch. He raised an eyebrow at her, his smile slightly crooked. Her skin began a fresh rash of itching along the backs of her thighs. "I'm okay. Truly."

The pastor nodded at her. "All right. The union of marriage is, of course, a holy triumvirate. The wife, the husband and the Lord."

Oh, boy. That was all she needed. What did the Lord think about marriages of convenience? Had that been done in the Bible? Surely yes. Surely she wasn't going onto the Bad Girl list because of their agreement?

I've got to quit worrying about that! I'm sure the Lord understands about ill mothers who believe they're on their deathbed. She removed her hand from Mitch's and clasped her fingers together tightly.

Gently, but insistently, he reached and took both her hands in his, holding her. Pastor Richardson beamed at him.

Crystal felt heat along the back of her neck. Great. Just great. Mitch had everybody in his corner—including, apparently, the angels and the Creator and every other holy entity who knew she was a big fake when it came to being a bride.

It's not too late to back out of this, a strangely soothing voice whispered tantalizingly in her ear.

Crystal jumped, positive Mitch and Pastor Richardson had heard the voice as well. It had been as clear as if Mitch had said the words in her ear. She frowned, wondering if he was communicating his thoughts by mental telepathy.

But no. His full attention was on the pastor's instructions. Miserably, Crystal realized she didn't even know the topic that was being discussed.

And then she knew that she was the one who was in danger of not showing up this time around.

The wrenching part of that knowledge was how much it would hurt Mitch. She couldn't hurt him. Not when he was already in so much pain.

Still, was her red and rashy body warning her that she was about to make the biggest mistake of her entire life? There was more to marriage than simply showing up for the ceremony. She was in danger of losing her heart to Mitch all over again— and he'd be the first to tell her that he wasn't in the business of taking care of hearts anymore.

AFTER THEY'D ENDURED ninety minutes of premarital counseling, Mitch and Crystal headed over to the Jennings's home to check on Bess.

"You're uncharacteristically quiet tonight," he commented as they walked up the sidewalk. "But I took notes for you in case you weren't paying attention to Pastor Richardson."

"I was paying attention," Crystal insisted.

"It's going to be all right," he told her, ignoring her blatant fib. "We're in this together."

"I'm trying to figure out exactly what we're in. It's been a long time since I've felt so…so unsettled in my life."

He laughed. "I'm going to kiss Aunt Elle tonight for getting us together again."

"It was my mother."

He stopped at the porch and took her in his arms. "Actually, it was mostly Aunt Elle. I had called over here that day to talk to you for old times' sake. I don't know," he said with a rueful smile. "Maybe I wanted to reconnect with someone who knew me before I became a surgeon. Someone who remembered me as a hopeful kid instead of a physician whose reputation is taking a hammering by a family who has every right to be angry."

"Oh, Mitch," she said softly. "You know you did everything you could. I know it, too."

"Yeah, but that doesn't change the outcome, does it?" He sighed heavily. "So I called over here to talk to you and Aunt Elle suggested I meet her down at your shop so that she could reintroduce us."

"Boy did she ever," Crystal murmured. "I'm not surprised that she was meddling. She is Mom's younger sister."

She gently pulled herself from Mitch's arms and opened the front door. Walking inside, they were greeted by Aunt Elle.

"I've been wondering if you two would make it tonight," she said, hugging them both. "I've kept dinner warm."

"We made it," Crystal said. *We made it through one more nerve-racking tunnel on the way to the altar of short-term commitment.* "Where's Mom?"

"Oh, resting, dear." Elle met her gaze with some reluctance. "She tired easily today."

Instantly, Crystal looked at Mitch, her eyes wide.

His gaze slid away.

She looked down, puzzled and worried and somehow angry with him. *He could just run up and check on her. That wouldn't cause him any undue stress.*

But she couldn't ask that of him. "Should I call the doctor and mention how she's feeling?"

"We'll see how she does after she rests."

They all three stood uncomfortably in the foyer for a long moment. Crystal recognized a stirring presence of resentment inside her which she knew was unfair and yet couldn't seem to help. Nobody was better than Mitch at knowing what the physical heart needed in order to heal! And yet he held back from this entire matter.

Commitment. Crystal wondered how much of that they would find themselves giving each other in the six weeks they planned to be married. *I'd feel so much better if he'd just offer to check on Mom!*

A big smile suddenly lifted Elle's delicately lined features.

"Come out to my studio," she said. "I have something I want to show you."

Mitch and Crystal dutifully followed, but she noticed that he didn't make a move to hold her hand or her shoulders as he normally did.

They stepped inside, and Elle turned on a pleasing low light. Crystal breathed deep. "I love it in here. It's so peaceful."

"That's what Sister says, too. And Martin hasn't

said it, but I find him in here occasionally inspecting my latest creations. Make yourself comfortable on that chaise," she instructed. "I have to check something in here."

Elle's petite figure disappeared into a small room off the main studio. Crystal sat, as did Mitch, though they didn't scat themselves close together on the lounge.

"I've never seen so much china," Mitch said softly. "It's all beautiful. She could have a large showing."

Crystal smiled. "I know. She has an amazing gift."

"Does she ever sell any of it?"

"Oh, no. She says working for money would hamper her artistic creativity. She has to do what she feels." Crystal thought about what she'd just said before sighing to herself. "She gives away a piece now and again for a charity auction or to a good friend whom she knows will enjoy it. Even I have only one piece, which she gave me when I opened my own store. I'm always bugging her about giving me another one." She smiled at Mitch. "I think that's why I was so delighted with the teacup I bought. Did you know that Kathryn handpainted it? And the dog bowl?"

He shook his head. "I noticed you always used the same teacup, but I didn't know it was her creation."

Crystal nodded. "Painting china is something Elle and Kathryn have in common."

She didn't say that Elle didn't paint as much as she used to, when Crystal had been in high school. Elle joked that she was getting old and couldn't see to paint as well, but Crystal thought that was probably an excuse so no one would ask her what she was working on at the present. It seemed almost every time she saw her aunt she was wearing her painting clothes. "When Aunt Elle dies, we're supposed to smash every single thing she's created in this room," she said softly.

"Smash it! Why?"

She smiled a little at the shock in Mitch's tone. "It's her greatest pride and joy to bring her talent to life. She finds it agonizing to think that one day her beautiful things could end up in a garage sale, pawed over by strangers."

"You would never sell her art! Surely she knows that."

"She does. But suppose something happened to me after my family was gone? People die, you know, and—" She broke off her words as she saw the wide-eyed, traumatized expression on Mitch's face. She gasped. "I'm sorry, Mitch! I didn't mean that to sound so casual!"

"It's okay," he muttered. But he looked away from her and she could see that his skin was pale around his eyes.

Of all the unfortunate, callous things for her to say. Crystal held back another apology and the instant desire she had to throw her arms around him and kiss the pain away. How could she have said something so thoughtless?

"You didn't mean anything by it," he murmured. "This is something I have to deal with on my own, Crystal. I know you're trying to help me, but the fact is, no one can."

Elle bounced back into the room, her face lit with excitement. "Come see!" she called gaily.

They went into the small room. Crystal gasped, and Mitch put his arm around her. A sixteen-place china setting lay displayed on top of a white, woven cloth. On shelves above, such things as a covered tureen and a sugar-creamer set shone with gleaming pride. It was all white with fabulous gold rims, and on each piece, intricate yet somehow elegant patterns of gold trailing flowers seemed to float with living joy.

"This is my wedding gift to you both," Elle said happily.

"Oh, my gosh," Crystal whispered. "However did you find the time to do all of this? It's stunning!" She picked up a teacup, turning it slowly in her palm so she could see every detail.

"I've been working on it little by little since the day you were born," Elle told her, a mischievous smile on her face. "And look!" She turned the teacup over in Crystal's palm. A tiny gold star was painted on the bottom of the cup. "When your mother named you Crystal Star, I created your own mark. I call it the Crystal Star, as a matter of fact, and it's on the bottom of every piece. You always were, you know, the light in our lives, Crystal, dear.'' She smiled up at both of them. ''And we're so delighted our girl is marrying a prince. It seems like a fairy tale come true to us.''

''I don't know what to say,'' Crystal murmured. She felt delight and joy and panic and distress all colliding inside her stomach as red heat flamed up her back. She didn't deserve this gift! All the years of hard work Elle had spent doing this out of the love in her heart for her niece, and Crystal wasn't being honest. If Aunt Elle wanted every piece of her private collection of china smashed when she died, then what would she want done with all this hard work when Crystal and Mitch divorced?

She could never smash this gift. Never.

Elle was staring at her curiously, waiting for her to say something. Mitch squeezed her shoulders, willing her to accept the loving gift. Shaking, Crystal looked down at the lovely cup with the beautifully shaped gold star on the bottom. ''It's something I've always dreamed of, Aunt Elle,'' she finally whispered, ''just to have one more piece. I'm overwhelmed that you've created my own pattern. I can't thank you enough. And this is the most beautiful china I've ever seen.''

And then she hugged her aunt close to her, holding her as tightly as she could. ''Thank you,'' she said. ''Thank you so much.''

Chapter Thirteen

"Ugh. I'm ill," Crystal told Mitch as they sat in front of the TV later that evening. Dogs and cats ignored them as they adopted their relaxed positions on the floor and bookshelves.

"I thought you didn't look so good at dinner. But it wasn't Elle's cooking. It was too delicious to be that." He had a bad feeling he knew what was bothering Crystal, and it was emotional rather than gastronomical. If he could get her through the next two nights, she'd be his, at least long enough to give him a shot at convincing her to stay married to him.

He'd had the most disquieting sensation all day that Crystal was hanging on to their wedding plans by the thinnest of threads. "Maybe you need rest. You've been doing a lot, and you've been worried about your family. Why don't we call it a night?"

Hesitantly, she looked at him. "Mitch, would you mind if I had these last two nights to myself?"

His stomach shifted alarmingly inside him. She was crawfishing on him! "Crystal, have I done something to upset you?"

"No, no," she said hastily. "I just feel a need to sleep alone until the big night." Her face turned a blanched hue as she struggled with her thoughts. "Isn't there something about bad luck to see the bride before the wedding or something?"

He frowned at her, not fooled by her excuse at all. "I'll go, of course, but I'll miss you."

Her lips parted, trembled. For a woman who claimed to be afraid that he wouldn't make it to the altar, she didn't seem very interested in keeping him at her side. "Maybe we *should* have bought handcuffs instead of rings," he said as lightly as possible. "I'm getting the strange feeling I'd be wise to attach you to my side."

"I'll be there," she said, her tone quiet and serious. "I admit to having massive nerves, though."

"Is that why you haven't chosen a dress?"

A very sweet blush he found quite charming stole up her neck.

"How did you know about that?"

He shrugged. "Janet and Genie mentioned they were playing bridal consultants. I am, of course, hoping that they do it differently than you do."

She grinned at him. "You mean somehow helping me to back out of our agreement?"

"I'd prefer a different result."

"Oh, Mitch. I know I'm doing the right thing. It's such a big, scary step, even if it is a short-term situation."

He wouldn't comment on that. "So did you like either of their choices?"

"I'm still thinking over the options."

His heart turned over inside him. She really was doing this out of love and compassion for her bed-ridden mother. He had hoped...

He made a pact with himself to do nothing to ever hurt her again. Perhaps in six weeks he could make serious headway into healing her pain. "Whatever you wear, you'll be a beautiful bride."

"I thought I'd feel differently," she murmured. "I must say I'm getting new insight into why so much stress walks in the door with every bride." She gave him a shy glance. "Are you nervous?"

He held up his hand, horizontally. "Not a tremor in me. Steady as a rock."

She took a deep breath. "Promise me that when we terminate our agreement, we won't be like poor Kathryn and Tom. I want to believe we'll always be friends no matter what, Mitch. I don't want us to be enemies."

He saw the shudder pass through her, and with dismay realized what was bothering her. "You mean, when the time is up, we part ways on friendly terms."

"I would hate knowing that we traded in a per-fectly good friendship for a few weeks of matri-monial camouflage."

He felt pretty certain she was asking if he would go peacefully out of her life, no strings attached, like the agreement she would have had with Bar-ney.

It would kill him to give her up again.

"I would never be like Tom," he said. "Is that what's got you so upset? Because you weren't upset when we agreed to get married."

"I know. I think Aunt Elle giving us her present tonight shook me up." She rubbed her arms, the bare skin goose-pimpled. "She put her whole heart into it because she believes we're forever. And we're deceiving them all."

He wasn't. He loved Crystal. He wanted a life-long commitment with her.

"I couldn't bring myself to break that china," she murmured.

You won't have to, he thought.

CRYSTAL CRAWLED INTO BED wearily. Igor, Thor and Nip cozied themselves into the positions in the bed they'd enjoyed before Mitch had encroached upon their space. Five cats found various places to drape themselves, two upon her pillow.

"You're glad he's gone," she said to her menagerie.

A cat yawned. Thor licked her hand.

"You don't seem all that glad." She scowled into the darkness. "I think you're fickle beasts. You don't know what you want."

Igor blew out a breath.

"You just want me to shut up so you can go to sleep." Crystal pulled the covers up against her chin. "The thing is, I think I miss him."

He'd held her hair when she'd been sick in the night. He cradled her close to his chest and soothed her to sleep. He made love to her like there was no tomorrow.

Only a couple of weeks ago, she'd had no hope of tomorrow with the man she'd never forgotten. Now, thanks to her family, tomorrow glimmered faintly on the horizon like a mirage, elusively within, yet out of reach.

"I'm such a case," she told her pets. "I've got basically one more day to think this through, and you're no help at all!"

BEFORE THE REHEARSAL, Crystal sat in the Red Horn Café with Janet and Genie. It was basically her bachelorette party, because she had insisted she didn't want one. So they'd kept it simple, just this meeting at the café.

It had turned into more of a nerve-soother, though. Sensing her distress, Genie and Janet kept her hot tea mug full and their ears open.

"You look pale," Janet commented.

"Kind of anxious," Genie said.

"Well, that's normal, isn't it?" Who was she kidding? She was about to jump out of her skin. If this was normal, how did anyone ever handle looking forward to marriage? "Can I ask you something, Genie?"

"Sure."

Crystal swallowed. "I don't mean to pry, but I did notice that you're not wearing your lip ring anymore. Did Linc ask you not to?"

"Oh, no." Genie laughed. "Linc says he doesn't

care one way or the other. I tried it on for him once, but he just shrugged. To tell you the truth, I felt kind of silly when the man I love was staring at the ring in my lip. I want to be beautiful for Linc. I don't need to be radical anymore. So,'' she said with a shrug, ''it became obvious to me that the ring was in my way. I want to get as close as I can to Linc when we're kissing. I don't want *anything* in the way.'' Her grin was saucy.

''I see.'' Crystal knew how heavenly it was to be in Mitch's arms. ''Your hair looks very pretty with the new color, although I liked the raspberry.''

Genie's eyes danced. ''My hair will always be short and sassy, but somehow I feel more beautiful to my lover with my natural black hair. Note the burgundy highlights, however.''

''It's lovely,'' Crystal murmured. ''What did Linc say about that?''

''That he loved me with pink hair, he'd love me with purple.'' She laughed out loud. ''He said he'd love me if I was bald, and somehow that led to an afternoon of lovemaking. I'm not sure how.''

They shared a conspiratorial giggle. Crystal looked at Janet, the questions still on her mind. ''Janet, I couldn't help noticing when I fit you for the ice-blue bridesmaid dress that you seem to…you seem to—''

''Have lost weight? I have.'' Janet's grin was as big as Genie's. ''The five pounds I added when I was worried about getting married somehow shed right off after I broke the engagement. I still talk to my former fiancé, and I'm glad we're friends of a sort, but I know now I was marrying him for acceptance. I mistook fondness for true love." She sat up proudly. "I'm starting a fitness routine, and I'm loving it!"

"A fitness routine?" Crystal asked carefully.

"As a matter of fact, yes. Frankie happened to jog by the house one day when I was out getting the mail. He asked me to join him, and I did. It's fun!"

Crystal lifted an eyebrow. "The jogging, or the company?"

"Oh, Frankie and I will always be just friends. In fact, he's dating a girl in Dallas he likes real well. But I'd forgotten how good it feels to be with a man simply for the sake of companionship. Somehow I feel more attractive, especially as I can tell I'm becoming more fit. And goodness knows, Frankie is an excellent fitness coach."

"So you're doing this for yourself? Not because you and your fiancé broke up?"

"Only for me. No one else."

"Oh, dear," Crystal said. "I'm so glad you figured it out in time. You look great."

"The point is, I feel great. It's something I've done for me, and no one else. Just like Genie getting rid of most of her rebel tendencies. She didn't do it because Linc asked her to. She wanted to. She rebelled by having fuschia hair and a lip ring and a fiancé who was all wrong for her, although truth to tell, that turned out to be a good thing because it brought Mitch riding home on his white charger to oust the evil fiancé. And then you two got together. Isn't it wonderful?''

"Yes," Crystal murmured. "I think so."

"Do you love him?" Genie asked.

Did she love Mitch? Of course she did. She always had.

"Let's not be deep tonight," Janet suggested. "Let's talk about the surprise gown Crystal has chosen."

She smile wanly. "I think you're going to be very surprised."

"How could you keep the secret from us?" Genie asked. "We're taking bets as to whether it's short or long."

"Oh, I hope it will be a long one," Crystal said softly, thinking about her impending marriage.

"You don't know yet?" Janet asked in alarm. "I thought we'd laid out some very attractive suggestions a few days ago. Even that was pushing it for tardiness, hon."

Crystal stirred her tea, focusing on her friends again. "Do you think that a long gown might predict a long marriage, and a short gown predict a short marriage?"

"Nope," Genie said decisively. "I wore a short dress, and Linc and I are totally forever."

"It's not like predicting the stock market," Janet said with a smile. "Although I never really believed that hem length fashions could affect whether the market went up or down."

"Of course, it couldn't hurt to build in a little good luck charm, I suppose." Genie grinned, as if quite proud of herself. "Baseball players have all kinds of superstitions, like not shaving before a big game or wearing dirt on their cap."

Janet narrowed her eyes on her little sister. "You're *not* suggesting we dust her veil with a little dirt or swipe her razor tomorrow? I'm pretty sure our brother would prefer we be a bit more civilized when it comes to our new sister-in-law." She beamed at Crystal.

Crystal swallowed. Her throat went tight.

"We're so excited that you're going to be our sister," Janet said, her pretty eyes glowing.

"And Mom and Dad are delirious, to say the least," Genie agreed. "At least one marriage in the family is going the traditional route."

Not quite. Crystal tried to smile. And then her smile turned real as she thought about being a part of Mitch's family. She truly liked his parents and his sisters. Maybe she wasn't such a huge fraud. They liked her and she liked them, and goodness knows, more had grown out of less than she and Mitch had, right? "I'm excited, too. In fact, I'm starting to get very excited about tomorrow."

Maybe all she'd needed was to know that their secret was safe. Or maybe it was simply knowing that everyone thought this marriage was the right thing to do. Her minister and these families had all known her and Mitch since they were kids. If they saw only good in what they were doing, well, then maybe there *was* only good in it.

Then she had nothing to fear.

"If you'll excuse me," she told them, "I've got an errand or two I must run before tonight."

"You'll be at the rehearsal, won't you?" Genie teased. "We have instructions to make certain you're there one way or the other, in whatever condition need be."

Crystal shook her head and leaned into the booth to hug each of them. "I'll be there."

But right now, she had a mission. It was time to revisit the past, and then let it go for good.

SHE SLIPPED INTO HER childhood home without alerting her family to her presence. They were probably resting up for the evening's rehearsal, and her mother especially needed all the sleep she could get before becoming a mother-of-the-bride. Without making a sound on the staircase, she went upstairs and over to the attic door, which she slowly opened.

Inside the attic were the mementoes every family kept hidden away among the occasional cobweb. Childhood treasures, old furniture they couldn't bear to part with, Uncle Martin's golf clubs, Bess's homecoming crown, Aunt Elle's batons.

Crystal smiled to herself and went over to the small closet against one wall. She opened it and turned on the light. Gasping, she reached out to touch the first A-line skirt she'd ever sewn—in high school as a home ec assignment—and the much better clothing results that had come after. Pinned to the garments were the ribbons she'd received as the A-line skirts became elaborate gowns and were entered in statewide contests. Crystal shook her head. She would never have known that all those cherished hours she'd spent designing would have resulted in her owning her very own bridal store. It was as if she'd always known what she wanted.

And I did, of course, she thought, coming to the last plastic-covered hanger hidden at the back of the closet. She didn't need a label on the outside of the bag to know what was inside. There was no ribbon. No grade received proudly posted and tied to the hanger. Forgotten, it waited for her to let it free from its protective cocoon.

"Not forgotten. Just put aside until the time was right," she murmured, unzipping the bag. Drawing out the gown, she marveled that the ecru color had stayed true, not deepening with age. The fashion was no longer the latest, but at the time, she had thought it so smart to create a long, slimming gown when other girls were wearing bell-shaped skirts. Hers had been off-the-shoulder, very garden party. Down the back, she'd sewn a scattering of golden leaves for a trailing effect.

She held it up to herself, wondering what Mitch would have thought if he'd seen her in the prom dress. In the corner of the attic was an old mirror, streaked with age and broken in frame, but she had spent many hours in front of it as a child trying on Elle's old hats. Standing in front of it, she held the gown up to her, almost waiting for the magic and excitement she'd felt in sewing it to come washing back over her. She had looked so forward to being with Mitch that she'd worked on this dress for hours, every seam holding her dreams and childhood fantasies in each stitch.

She looked—and saw nothing but a faded dress being held by a mature woman.

It wasn't a good color on her, she realized. The ecru washed her out. Why had she chosen the material? In the store, it had seemed so different from the sherbet pastels she knew her friends were wearing. The dress was pretty, but she was taller now, more filled-out, no longer a young girl.

She sighed with happiness. "It was an A effort," she said out loud, "but you really belong on someone else."

A throat cleared behind her, and she whirled. "Oh, hi, Uncle Martin. I was just going through some old things," she said, hurriedly stuffing the dress back in its bag.

"Putting away some childhood toys?" he asked, his voice kind and understanding.

"I think so. It wasn't easy to face it, but now that I have, I know that everything turned out for the best."

He smiled, the skin crinkling around the eyes. "I'd say you'd feel more like a bride in something more suited to the holy occasion."

She closed the closet door and turned to face

him. "I'm feeling distinctly like tons of sequins and maybe a handful of beads."

He put out his arms, and she walked into his embrace.

"I think I saw something down at your shop that fits that description. If we hurry, I can help you pin the skirt for length, and I'm no slouch at sewing on a few extra beads, either."

"Who would have ever thought time in the marines would have taught you so much about fine sewing?"

"Nah. I learned to sew in the marines, but having a little princess in the house taught me about fine things. You did see that I saved all your ribbons and awards, didn't you?"

She nodded happily. "I thought you'd let Mom take the credit for storing away all the memorabilia."

"No way. She's not that organized. The prom dress was the only one she stored, and it lacks an identifying label. I'd say that's appropriate, though, wouldn't you?"

She nodded, her head against his shoulder.

"Well, come on, then. Let's get started on the most beautiful wedding gown Lover's Valley has ever seen!"

Chapter Fourteen

Mitch wasn't nervous as he waited at the altar for his bride. She'd suffered nerves, he knew, even to the point of remarking that she was lucky her stressed condition hadn't shown up on her face. But he thought she was beautiful. He was early to the church, and had sent a message back to the bride so she could see he had only gotten away from her once.

This time, they were going to spend the evening dancing at their wedding reception.

The gymnasium was beginning to fill with family and friends. Apparently, no one planned on missing what had swiftly become "the" June wedding.

"Ready?" Linc asked him.

"Ready."

"Still time to give her to me," Barney invited. "I've always had a peculiar itch for that li'l gal."

"Don't think so," Mitch said with a grin. "Anyway, I thought I'd noticed you particularly itching for another lady lately."

Barney flushed, his round features shining with secret happiness. "Could be."

"I'd take Crystal off your hands," Frankie offered. "Wouldn't want you suffering unduly. She can be a handful, you know."

Did he ever. In all the right places, too. He clapped his friend on the back. "She says I'm stuck with her, fellows. Guess I'll have to bear my fate in silence."

"Yep," Linc said with a satisfied sigh. "Not another word after 'I do.'" His gaze found Genie as she darted through a doorway leading to where the ladies were getting dressed. "Actually, I gotta say it's pretty nice to just shut up and let my body do the talking."

The men guffawed, engaging in more back-slapping repartee.

"After all these years of you being a big mouth, you let a little bitty girl shut you up?" Mitch teased.

Linc grinned. "I sure did. You wait and see if you'd rather talk, or listen to what a big strong man you are when your wife is riding the rollercoaster of lovemaking."

Mitch raised his eyebrows and did his best not to laugh at big Linc so clearly tamed by tiny Genie. "I'm glad you find my sister to be a suitable wife," he said, somewhat primly.

Barney and Frankie let out snickers not appropriate for usherlike behavior. But the look on Linc's face was reverent.

"Oh, she is," he said. "She's the only woman worth the big touchdown."

Well, Mitch thought, that wasn't quite how he'd describe his soon-to-be bride, but he had a feeling the label didn't matter.

His face fell as he thought about the duration of their marriage. Six weeks of life with Crystal was too short. Why had he agreed to that? Because a little of her was better than nothing, and nothing was all he'd had for years? Because he was hoping to change her mind?

He'd made it to the altar without a hitch. All he could do from here was show her how much he loved her.

He had always loved Crystal, and he always would. There was nothing convenient about the way he loved that lady. She might be a cynic when it came to romance, but he had six weeks to turn her into a believer.

CRYSTAL WAS GLAD to hear that Mitch was greeting guests in the gymnasium. It calmed her shivers to a mere tremor of excitement. "I'm really getting married!" she said to Kathryn. "It's really happening!"

Kathryn smiled, although it wasn't the bright smile from her cheerleader days Crystal associated with her friend. "You're a lovely bride, Crystal. I know this will all work out for you."

Crystal halted, putting down a lipstick. "Are you feeling okay?" She suddenly realized that Kathryn not only wasn't smiling, her personality was down a watt or two.

"I'm fine."

But her voice lacked the sparkling luster it normally had. Crystal began to be concerned. "Is the baby sleeping at night? Are you getting enough rest?"

"I think being a little tired goes along with new parenthood." Kathryn shook her head. "I feel fine mostly."

"I'm not a good person to dispense advice to new mothers," Crystal murmured. "I'm barely one to advise new brides. We're not leaving immediately for our honeymoon. Why don't you let Mitch and I keep the baby tomorrow night so you can get some rest?"

Kathryn laughed. "A hideous thing to do to a newly wedded couple. Trust me, it's very difficult to build a marriage when there's a little one crying, and I would think even more difficult if the child isn't yours." She kissed Crystal's cheek and began arranging her hair in a beguiling upsweep of loose curls "Anyway, I'm much better than I ever was."

Crystal looked down at her hands. She felt so sorry for Kathryn she didn't know what to do. "I wish it had worked out for you and Tom."

"Oh, don't be sorry for me." Kathryn's artful fingers pulled the blond strands of hair this way and that as she took bobby pins from a case. "Marriage has to be fifty-fifty. To be truthful, it has to be one hundred-one hundred percent. Both of us had to be willing to put in one hundred percent desire for it to work.'' She shrugged. "I'm through with worrying why it went wrong. My baby has erased all that from my mind. I'm a great parent, if I do say so myself.''

Crystal smiled. "You were always great at everything. Most Popular, Most Likely to Succeed, Most Beautiful—''

"Just goes to show you that the past isn't necessarily a barometer for the future, doesn't it?''

Crystal's gaze met Kathryn's in the mirror. "I've been thinking that lately myself.''

Kathryn nodded. "Remember. One hundred percent, if it's going to work.''

They'd agreed on fifty-fifty. Crystal frowned, wondering if maybe they'd short-changed their chances from the start. "What would you say if I told you that Mitch and I aren't having a conventional marriage?'' she asked suddenly.

"Who does?'' Kathryn said with a shrug. "All marriages are defined by the people who decide to be joined together. Stop frowning. You don't want lines between your eyebrows at the altar.''

Crystal turned on the seat to face her friend. "Mitch and I are only staying married for six weeks.''

"Well,'' Kathryn said, forcibly turning Crystal back around on the linen-covered seat, "you're going to have a great hairdo, anyway, if you'll sit still.''

"You're not paying attention.''

"I am. I think you're paying too much attention to the wrong things. Focus is important in a marriage."

She raised her eyebrows. "I don't understand what you're saying."

"I'm saying that I've known you all your life. You've always been a stickler for details. It's what makes your gowns creations rather than mere stock. Details. Details. But you can drive yourself nuts with details, Crystal. Today is the happiest day of your life. Don't examine it like it's crystal beading. Just enjoy it."

"And then?"

"And then rip out the seams if it doesn't fit. But don't get out the seam ripper before it's time, hon. Nothing's written in nonerasable ink except the signatures on the wedding certificate, right?"

"Oh. You may have a point." She was quiet for a moment. "I'm surprised you feel the way you do, somehow."

Kathryn laughed. "Because my husband walked out on me? Well, maybe it is surprising I feel this way." She finished with the last delicate curls framing Crystal's face and gave the upswept hair a light spraying. "I didn't know it wasn't going to work out between Tom and me, but I'm not going to turn cynical about marriage. If I found the right man, I'd say yes in a flash."

"You would?"

"Sure. Why not? I got the best end of our deal, after all. Tom gets a new wife, but I got the baby."

She smiled luminously. "So what have I got to be cynical about? The baby may be keeping me up at night, but believe me, the not-exhausted part of me welcomes those quiet moments with my little daughter."

"I'm so glad to hear you say that. I've been so worried about you." She turned on the seat to face her friend. "I must not be as strong as you are, because I definitely don't think I'd be feeling the way you do. I'd be too mad at the jerk who walked out on me."

"You have a more forgiving nature than you think. You forgave me, didn't you?"

"Yes, but there was nothing to forgive. It wasn't your fault."

Kathryn smiled. "Sure it was, Crystal. I didn't want to go to the prom alone. I wanted to be crowned queen, and I wanted to be escorted if my name was called. I was pregnant and scared and feeling sorry for myself, and I made a bad decision. When your mother said you were sick and suggested I ask Mitch to go with me, I jumped at the chance without asking you how you felt about it. Of course, I never dreamed that…that you were waiting for him to show up. You can't know how much I've regretted that night over and over again. A pretend crown isn't worth losing a friend over."

Crystal shook her head. "I don't regret it at all. My mother was right. Mitch and I were too serious. We might have simply gotten married and settled down in Lover's Valley and never achieved the things we did. He's a renowned surgeon. I wouldn't take that from him for anything.'' She sighed. ''We probably wouldn't be getting married today because we would have never made it from high school all the way through med school. Everything turned out for the best.''

''See? You even forgave Mitch. That's what makes you so special, Crystal. You're not really a cynic at all. You just want so badly to keep yourself from getting hurt again. But I don't think there's going to be a lot of pain in your marriage to Mitch. I've never seen two people more destined to be together.''

Crystal smiled. ''Sometimes it feels that way. Sometimes I actually believe it myself.''

''That's what's carrying you to the altar, then. And that's what will keep you and Mitch together, if that's what you want to happen. Neither of you signed the six-week thing in blood, so act like you didn't agree to it. What's up with six weeks, anyway?''

The lightheartedness left Crystal, sucking the warmth out of her. She shivered in her satin robe. ''My mother wanted desperately for me to get married. So she had the party for me, only she must have had a preexisting heart condition. I think she overworked herself trying to get me married off, but she says that's nonsense. The truth is, my unmarried state at this point grieves her deeply.''

Kathryn laughed out loud.

''It's really not funny,'' Crystal told her. ''Once

my mother's got an idea in her head, it's carved on a stone tablet!''

"Okay, okay. I know how much your mother loves you. Go on.''

"Well, then this heart thing came up. She was convinced it was guilt.'' Crystal shook her head. "When she found out she needed surgery, she became even more distressed. About everything. And convinced she was destined to be turning up the daisies shortly. By then my unmarried state was really worrying her.''

Kathryn giggled, seating herself on the bench next to Crystal. "And then what?''

"She wanted Mitch to do the surgery, but he...he couldn't.'' Crystal didn't want to divulge Mitch's demons on that subject, so she glossed over it. "Positive that only Mitch could save her life, Mom really began playing the guilt harp. We agreed to get married to calm her down and give her a healthy outlook through the surgery and recovery period.'' She gave Kathryn a sidelong glance. "Because you know the minute she heard the word *wedding* she was positive grandbabies were next.''

"I'm sure that was the plan,'' Kathryn said with a grin. "But why six weeks?''

"Mitch said that if she was going to have a healthy outcome from the balloon procedure, we'd know fairly quickly after the surgery. If it wasn't sufficient to unblock her arteries, then she'd go in for more extensive surgery. We wanted her mind at peace in case the worst scenario presented itself. Six weeks seemed like a good amount of time.''

''And then what? You were going to break her heart by splitting up? After you gave her something to recover for?''

Crystal's lips turned down a little. ''That does sound cruel, doesn't it?''

''A little.'' Kathryn shook her head. ''I don't think she'd ever believe you two weren't meant for each other. It seems she would just go into high-gear manipulation to keep you two together. I'm talking maximum guilt trip here, and maybe passion-inducing drugs sprinkled into yours and Mitch's food.''

Crystal gasped.

''No, maybe not the passion-inducing drugs,'' Kathryn said on a laugh, ''but I don't think she'd give in easily. I don't see divorce papers in your future, Crystal.''

Crystal's lips twisted. ''I don't know if that's such a bad thing,'' she said softly.

''Trust me, they're ugly documents. All these cold, legal terms and pages and pages of stipulations about everything you can imagine. It's almost like splitting your breath down the middle.''

''Stop!'' Crystal clutched her robe tighter. ''Kathryn, I'm so sorry!''

''Don't be, because next time I wear a wedding gown, you're selling it to me and I'm going to be smiling from ear to ear, the happiest bride you ever saw.''

"Really?" Crystal perked up. "Any man I know?"

"Maybe. Well, of course you know him. This is Lover's Valley, after all. We've all known each other forever."

"Not you and Barney," Crystal said on a breath. "He said he'd never settle down!"

Kathryn gave her a mysterious look as they sat together on the linen-covered bench. "He said you said that, too. Now, one of you either wasn't listening to your own words, or your mind got changed somehow."

Crystal smiled. "My mind got changed."

Kathryn nodded at her. "There's nothing carved in stone that says his can't get changed, too."

She had to laugh at that. "I suppose if I can be taking a walk down the aisle, it can happen to Barney Fearing, too." She shivered with happiness. "I'm actually beginning to believe that all my dreams can come true."

"You've waited a long time for yours, Crystal. You're making the right choice. Life is about making good choices, most of the time." Kathryn sighed and touched her fingers to her forehead briefly, as if she had a headache.

Crystal frowned. Kathryn didn't feel well, but she obviously didn't want to talk about it. Having a new baby and very little support had to be exhausting.

"So. You haven't told me what Mitch's getting out of this arrangement."

Crystal looked at her.

"If you agreed to marry him for your mother's benefit, what does he get out of it?"

"Oh. Respectability, he said." A smile lit Crystal's face. "Not that I would equate marrying me with gaining respectability. But he says it helps to have a wife and family in his practice."

"He's done all right so far without one," Kathryn observed. "Does it have anything to do with the negligence suit being pursued against him?"

Crystal started as she turned to look in Kathryn's eyes. "How did you know about that?"

Kathryn shrugged. "Everyone knows. This is Lover's Valley. How does one keep a secret in this town?"

They didn't, not forever, anyway. "Mitch would be so upset," Crystal murmured. "Oh, dear. If he knew everyone out there in the gym has been talking about something he can't even talk much about, it would be very embarrassing for him." She thought about that for a minute. "I'm not going to tell him. Maybe later, but not anytime soon."

"I'm sure he knows people have heard by now. Why else would marrying you for 'respectability' make sense?"

Crystal's eyes widened.

"No one cares about the lawsuit, Crystal. Mitch will always be a hometown hero in Lover's Valley's eyes. He should know that."

"I don't think he does. He's very ashamed."

"Well, then." Kathryn stood. "Marrying you today is going to make him feel a lot better." She reached for a makeup bag and began to dust some powder over Crystal's face.

Crystal sat still, allowing Kathryn to do as she liked. Inside, her heart tore a little as she thought over her friend's words. Since he didn't want to talk about how he felt about not operating again, she avoided bringing up the issue. So she'd allowed herself to forget the part about him marrying her for the happy family portrait and the respectability. Wrapped up in her dreams, she'd forgotten about the reality—they both had something to gain in this marriage.

And she'd allowed her feelings to blossom and grow, nurtured by impractical happiness and emotions that felt new and good to her starved soul.

It would hurt far more to sign divorce papers than it had to be left behind on prom night, she realized. And she had no one to blame but herself for dreaming of something that wasn't to be—a second time.

THE CRAZY THING WAS, when Crystal finally said "I do," she was torn between laughing and crying. She was crying because part of her was so happy, and laughing because she knew it was ridiculous to be crying with joy. It was an arrangement, after all. The conflicting sentiments made her shake so that her veil trembled around her face and her hands rattled the white rose bouquet she held. So when she said the words finalizing her acceptance of

Mitch as a husband, it came out in a whisper, only audible to Mitch and Pastor Richardson.

"Was that legal and binding?" Mitch asked Pastor Richardson. "Only you and I heard her. Maybe later she'll claim she really didn't marry me at all. Let's make her say it again."

Crystal shook harder, the laughter and tears almost painful as she tried to take a breath. "I'm barely hanging on here, Mitch. Let's not redo the entire ceremony."

He pushed her veil back so he could touch her cheek. "I want the time we have together to be real."

She took in a soft breath, a light gasp of surprise. But behind the surprise was pleasure at his words. "I do," she said more loudly, so that the entire congregation in the gymnasium clearly heard her vow. Why not be brave and throw herself completely out on that limb without the safety net below? If heartache was a monster in the closet, then she vowed to throw the doors wide open and stare her fear in the face. After all, Kathryn faced far more and survived with a smile on her face.

Crystal was strong. She'd simply never really allowed herself to be tested.

"I really, *really* do," she repeated, feeling strength build inside her as she broke free from the past.

Chapter Fifteen

Crystal threw her bouquet with straight aim, and it landed in a squealing Janet's arms. She waved it triumphantly, then pressed it to her nose before removing half the white roses from the gold cord with which they were tied and handing them to Kathryn.

"What's this for?" Kathryn asked.

"Because you're unmarried," Janet shot back. "Why else? Crystal's wedding bouquet *has* to be good luck. If she can get married—"

"It can happen to anyone," Kathryn said, finishing her sentence.

They laughed and posed for pictures. Mitch was ready for his part. He marched up to his bride, who appeared to have suddenly developed an attack of shyness. She stared up at him, her eyes huge with laughter, but some trepidation.

"This is the good part," he told her.

"How so?"

"I get to run my hand up your leg," he said with a grin. "If memory serves me correctly, you have great legs."

"It's nice to know that your memory isn't dulled by two days' absence from me," she retorted on a laugh.

"Absence makes the heart grow fonder. And it is my fondest wish to lift your skirt, Crystal McStern."

She sucked in a breath. "Oh, dear. That does sound…different, doesn't it?"

He cocked his head at her. "Just trying it on for size. I want to ease you into this marriage thing slowly."

"Good. I was never one to rush into things without a good push, which is why we're here today, I suppose." She smiled up at her groom.

"Lucky for me you didn't feel a need to do anything rash, like getting married right out of high school to some jock," he murmured against her hair. "Are you happy, Crystal?"

"Strangely enough, I am." She ran her fingers along his wrist, enjoying the strength and texture of his lightly haired skin. "Are you?"

"Strangely enough, I am." He squeezed her to him, to let her know he was teasing. "This feels like old times," he whispered, drawing her more tightly against him as they began to sway gently to the sounds of the string quartet he'd hired to play in the old gym. "I remember how much I loved dancing with you at the Sock Hop, and the Valentine's Day dance. I remember thinking how much I wanted to hold you, and take your clothes off of you, even though it took me a whole year to figure out how to achieve that goal. Like now, I get excited thinking about touching your leg to remove your garter. Isn't that crazy?''

''No,'' she said breathlessly. ''I'm so nervous it feels like you're going to take off my wedding gown instead of the silly old garter.''

''You turn me on,'' he whispered into her ear. ''You always did.''

''You're making me blush,'' she whispered back urgently. ''Everyone's going to know what we're talking about!''

''What else is a husband supposed to talk to his new wife about? World peace? Nuclear testing? We have years to discuss everything we want to.''

The minute he said it, he felt her jerk with surprise in his arms. ''Oops,'' he said, opening his eyes to stare down at her. ''I forgot. Never mind.''

She smiled shyly. ''There's nothing written in stone that it has to be six weeks,'' she said hesitantly. ''We could always have an open-ended understanding.''

''Hmm,'' he said, pretending to think it over, despite the fact that his heart was racing and his mind was screaming *Yes! She really does want me!* ''Open-ended could be good. We could negotiate something, I'm sure.''

She lay her head back against his chest. ''Since we have such pressing matters to discuss, we may need extra time.''

He tipped her chin so that he could brush her lips with his. ''I'm sorry if I misled you,'' he said huskily. "I don't plan on spending very much of our open-ended marriage talking. I have much better things I want to do with my wife."

He felt her shiver. His body answered with a shock wave of anticipation.

"Hey, McStern, where's the garter, man? Give one of us a chance!"

Mitch smiled down at Crystal. "The natives are restless. They want some of what I've got."

She raised her eyebrows. "A garter?"

"A wonderful woman," he told her, reaching for her skirt to draw it up to her knee. She balanced against his shoulder, and he took his time feeling the softness of her soft, slender thighs.

"It's not that far up," she said on a laugh, quivering as she tried to retain her balance. "Go south, young man."

"Too bad." He grinned and raised his eyebrows while the unattached males in the audience hooted and catcalled. "All right. Watch my aim."

He slid the garter from her leg, positioned it on his finger and shot it squarely at Barney, who caught it as unerringly as he'd always caught passes.

"I haven't lost any of my mo'!" Barney shouted, holding the garter up. "I can still catch a pass in heavy traffic!"

He put it over his suit, showcased his muscular biceps, posed for a fast picture, then snagged Kathryn from where she stood not too many feet away. They waltzed off to center floor, gazing at each other. The audience burst into applause, and Mitch grinned down at Crystal.

"I think we've started something."

She looked up at him. "I'm not certain exactly what we've started, but I'd have to agree with you." Some guilt curled into her as she saw the happy faces in the crowd around them, watching her and Mitch dance. *Should I tell him what Kathryn said? No. This many people wouldn't have shown up today if they'd thought Mitch had done something wrong.*

These people were their friends, had known them for years.

Yet, she had a feeling Mitch's happiness would be spoiled if he knew his secret was out. Unhappily, she watched as he accepted congratulations from an elderly couple who were friends of his family. His parents were on the fringes of the dance floor, talking to guests as if they were enjoying the evening. If Mitch had come home for a while to sort himself out and hide from the pressure, he had come to the wrong place.

As his wife, didn't she owe him the truth?

Maybe being a temporary wife gave her an out.

Coward! she accused herself.

Never again, she told herself. Mitch was happy. She wasn't going to shatter his happiness tonight. It couldn't possibly matter—much.

"I hope you don't mind waiting two days to leave for our honeymoon," he said in her ear.

"Not at all," she said lightly. He'd told her that

he was due in court for a preliminary hearing Monday. They would leave that night instead. "One stressful event in a day is enough."

"Getting married was stressful?" His voice held a teasing note.

"A little," she admitted. "Although it was better than I thought it would be."

"Better? Better? That's how you describe what most women say is the happiest day of their lives?"

She gave him an arch look. "I am not a typical woman, nor bride for that matter. And it was better to have one major event a day to focus on, so I'm actually glad we're enjoying our wedding night at home. I still have some things to pack."

"A bikini, I hope."

"I'm pretty sure you're aware that I'm not a bikini kind of girl."

He shifted her more securely in his arms. "Nudie?"

"Ah, the ever-hopeful male. Sorry. I'll be wearing a one-piece suit in Key West and down through the Bahamas."

"There's always the night, then."

"You want me to wear a bikini to bed?"

He chuckled. "I want you nude."

"Ahem."

Mitch and Crystal both turned at the sound meant to get their attention. It was the elderly couple who had congratulated Mitch a moment before.

"It's past our bedtime," Mr. Cowling said. "I

didn't want to leave without telling you to give 'em hell.''

Mitch smiled at Crystal. "Thanks. I'll try to take your sage advice tonight."

The elderly couple looked perplexed for a moment, then the wife whispered something into her husband's ear. "Oh. I get it. I don't think you'll be needing any wedding-night advice from me," he said with a big grin. "I mean on Monday."

Beneath her fingers, she could feel the muscles in Mitch's shoulders tense. His smile turned somewhat forced. "Monday?"

"At the hearing," Mrs. Cowling said quietly. "We're rooting for you, Mitch. Everything's going to come out just fine."

His smile was completely gone now. "How did you know about the hearing?"

"Oh, everybody knows," Mr. Cowling said. "And we're all behind one of our number one sons."

"Thank you." Mitch nodded at Mr. Cowling. "And thank you for coming tonight."

"Let us know how it goes," Mrs. Cowling called as Mitch moved Crystal back out onto the floor.

"I'm sure she'll hear," he said under his breath, though he waved politely at the departing couple. "Sometimes I think this town is filled with busybodies!"

"It is, Mitch. Remember, you've just married into a family full of them."

He focused on her. "Do you think Bess told people about the hearing?"

Crystal stiffened. "I didn't tell her, so I doubt she knows. And she wouldn't gossip about you, Mitch."

"Let's not bet the house on that."

"What are you saying?" Crystal could feel indignation beginning to bubble inside her.

"We're talking about a woman who deliberately sabotaged me on our prom date," he reminded her.

"Mitch, that's not fair! My family wouldn't do a thing to hurt you, or your family. They were trying to protect both of us, and my mother has bent over backward trying to make up to us for what she did."

"I know." He sighed heavily. "I'm sorry. I shouldn't have snapped at you like that. I was very surprised that the Cowlings knew, is all."

She stared at him unhappily. "Mitch, I don't think the lawsuit is a secret."

"What are you talking about?"

"Kathryn mentioned tonight that everyone here knows about it. News travels fast in Lover's Valley, and—"

"Kathryn knows, too?" His hands loosened on her, as if he wanted to walk right off the floor and escape. He glanced around the room.

"And I didn't tell her. I didn't tell anyone. Anyway, does it matter, Mitch?"

"Yes, it matters," he stated, his voice flat. "It matters, Crystal, more than you can know."

Hurt, she drew back a little. Of course. He'd married her in order to have the picture of respectability he needed. That's what she had agreed to do for him. It was her part of the bargain. Obviously, being married during a lawsuit provided him with a more stable persona; hence the haste for the wedding. Of course the expected honeymoon could come later; that was the least important aspect of their relationship.

"Oh, dear," she murmured, feeling the hives she'd thought conquered heat along her back. Uncomfortable warmth spread along her neck and zipped down her hips.

"Are you all right?" he asked. "You suddenly look…as if you might faint."

"No, I won't faint. I won't faint," she reminded herself. *And I won't cry, and I won't be crushed, and I won't tell myself how stupid I was to believe that this time, all my dreams would come true.*

"How is the bridal couple?" Bess called, coming to stand beside them. "Ready for the rice shower as you run out the door? Rice signifies luck for fertility, you know," she told them merrily, "and believe me, I made enough rice bags for the guests to throw that I'm positive it would fill a bushel basket. A bushel of babies! That has a nice ring, doesn't it?"

Chapter Sixteen

"I didn't think we'd ever get away," Mitch said on a groan. "I'm pretty sure I have rice lodged in my ear and embedded in my scalp."

"My mother has excellent aim," Crystal agreed. "One grain hit my tooth and it felt like she'd thrown a rock!"

"Your aunt Elle is no slouch with her aim, either. I think she dented the car with one handful. I'm taking the car into the shop next week and see if I can claim hail damage. You don't think they can run a test to tell the difference between hail and rice damage, do you?"

She shook the long skirt of her lovely wedding gown so that the rice would fall from the folds onto the living room carpet. The sequins and crystal beads danced in the light from the ceiling fixture, and for just an instant, she thought she saw the skirt twinkle with extra energy. Of course it was the effect of light on satin; there was nothing extraordinary nor magical about a woman's wedding gown.

"Mom's and Elle's enthusiasm was certainly showing."

He shook rice out of his hair. "Did they say something about rice affecting fertility in a positive way? I definitely thought I heard something to that effect, right before I was rice-blasted. Is rice a good luck charm, or is that one of those old wives' tales that have great underlying truth?"

Crystal decided it was best to shy away from the subject of fertility. "Probably rice only helps fertility if you scoop it up off the ground and take it home to boil up and snack on during the honeymoon. The groom would need to keep his strength up somehow, I suppose. Rice has stick-to-your-ribs qualities."

He tugged her hand. "Let's get back and start scooping, then. I'm famished!"

"I'm sure there's something in the kitchen you can forage for." She pulled her hand from his and picked up her skirt, heading toward her bedroom.

He caught her hand to turn her around. "Hey. Where are you off to?"

Her breath caught in her chest as she stared into his eyes. "I'm going to change."

"This minute?"

She raised her eyebrows. "Yes, this minute."

"Couldn't it wait a little while?" He turned her slowly around. "I really haven't had a chance to admire you."

The familiar tremor zinged up her legs and ran into her stomach, tightening it. Why did he have to look at her with such fire in his eyes? It made hope spring to life inside her; it made her heart beat faster with hopefulness! "You've seen me every night, Mitch. There's nothing more to admire."

"Oh, but there is." He reached out to gently touch her veil with one finger. "This is very soft."

She moved his hand away from the fairy tulle fabric. "Yes."

He touched the satin of the skirt. "And this is very soft."

She stepped back fractionally, so that her skirt was out of reach of his fingers. "Satin is a soft fabric," she said cautiously.

"And this is very soft," he said, stepping near to stroke her cheek. "And your lips are soft. Can I kiss you, Crystal?" he asked huskily.

The fact that he'd asked her permission caused her to hesitate. Had he sensed the barricade she had erected and wanted her to invite him to assault her senses? "I...don't know," she said, her voice a choked whisper.

He stepped nearer, his body pressing the skirt against her so that there was very little barrier left between them. "Why not? A groom should kiss his beautiful bride. I should kiss you." He enfolded her into his arms, sighing with what sounded like utter pleasure. "You feel made for me, almost a special order bride." Running a thumb lightly along her cheekbone, he swept along her lip in gentle, mesmerizing whisper-strokes. "I want to be your special order groom."

You are! she wanted to say. No other man could ever fit her the way he did; no other man could ever make her so happy. Even in high school when other girls were fickle, she only had eyes for Mitch McStern. He was her dream come true. "Did we want to marry each other, so we used Mother and a marriage of convenience as an excuse?" she asked. "Did we simply need each other?"

"I've asked myself that, too. Did I rationalize what we were doing because I wanted you so badly, and I knew the only way to get such a stubborn, set-in-her-ways young lady to the altar was by emotional luring? Was I trying to be your hero just so I could see my ring on your finger?" He rubbed his nose lightly against hers. "These are the wrenching questions that keep me up in the middle of the night."

"Oh, stop!" She laughed, giving him a slight slap on the arm as she stepped away from him. "You're back, Mitch McStern. You're back one hundred percent."

His brow crooked. "What do you mean I'm back? I never left."

"Oh, you did." She scooped her skirt over one arm and went into the kitchen to pour two glasses of champagne. "Your bedside manner is very wacky, normally. But when you're upset, the humor is replaced by this stern, cold male."

"Oh, like Dr. Jekyll and Mr. Hyde! I kind of like that. They were heroes of mine. Dr. Jekyll for the medicine, and Mr. Hyde for the patience to cope."

"You have no idea what you're talking about whatsoever. Did you ever see the movie? Help me pop this cork."

"Absolutely." He took the bottle from her and wrested the cork so that a silent puff of smoke filtered from the bottle. Pouring two glasses, he held one up for her to take. "No, I never saw the movie, so I'm teasing you, but I am willing to stay more light than dark whenever possible. I didn't mean to scare you."

She put down her glass. "I wasn't scared. I was…worried."

"Wasn't sure who you were marrying, huh? Worried you'd have to spend your life sleeping with a mad doctor? I know you weren't worried that I wouldn't show. I was at the gym this morning before they opened it."

"Mitch! I was worried about you. I don't know how to help you. I don't know very much about you, and we were going at this so quickly, I felt very lost."

He put her glass back into her hand and held his up. "I promise to always leave a trail of crumbs so that you can find your way back out when your husband turns into an impenetrable forest."

She smiled wryly. "You make it so hard to be serious."

"Laughter is the best medicine."

"For you, or for me?"

"For both of us. For our marriage."

She nodded. "All right." They clinked glasses

and each sipped some champagne. "Now, let me toast you in comparable fashion."

"I'm all ears."

She rolled her eyes. "Not last time I checked. Now, let me think of a suitable toast for you...all right. I hope that you'll always be glad you married me, even when I gripe that you leave the toilet lid up—"

"I do not! I did it once, and Thor decided he wanted a libation, so I've been extra-vigilant about that. I even posted a sign that says I don't drink out of your bowl, don't drink out of mine at doggie-level!" he said indignantly.

"And when I leave the toothpaste cap off, I promise to—"

"Never mind about toothpaste caps. They're small in the overall scheme of things. Get to the stuff that matters. I toasted you something important."

"Okay." She raised her eyebrow. "Here's to that smiling family portrait you wanted for your office hallway. I hope it brings you all the respectability you ever dreamed of, and may no one ever draw mustaches on it."

He laughed. They sipped their champagne and then he took her glass to set it on the counter. "You'd look good in a mustache. Didn't Lucy Ricardo wear one once?"

"Yes, but I'd rather not."

"Okay. You don't have to. I was only trying to make you feel better in case someone ever does put a mustache on the family portrait." He slid her into his arms.

"You don't think any of your patients ever would, do you?" she asked, her eyes closed, lulled by his nearness and their gentle teasing.

"It depends," he whispered against her earlobe. "After the hearing, a mustache may be the least of what is drawn on us."

She froze, then gently pulled out of his arms. He tried to pull her back but she shook her head. "Don't, Mitch."

"What's wrong?"

"Your mind is occupied by Monday, and I understand that. You don't really feel like…romance, and I don't want it when I know that you're thinking about something else. Let's wait until our hearts are in it."

The smile slipped from his face. He sighed. "I'm so sorry, Crystal. I wanted tonight to be everything you would have ever dreamed of for your wedding night."

"I knew what I was doing when I married you, Mitch. We set the table ahead of time, and there's no point in complaining about eating the meal now." She leaned up to give him a fast kiss on the lips. "Thank you for trying, though. It means a lot to me."

She turned and escaped down the hall into her bedroom. Not her bedroom, theirs now.

Theirs, because they'd agreed to it—for six weeks.

Why had she let herself forget that?

"Wait," he said, coming into the bedroom just as she realized she'd never be able to get herself out of her own wedding gown. There had to be fifty crystal bead buttons securing the back of her dress, and she could only reach the ones at the bottom of the skirt. She'd known the beading was slightly impractical, because it would take someone five minutes to help her into the gown, and five minutes to get her out. But she'd loved the old-fashioned feel of the minute buttons, and she'd loved how they glowed in the three-way mirror in the salon. Uncle Martin had assured her that the expensive, princess look of the gown was perfect for her.

Crystal had never considered that maybe she wouldn't want Mitch to have to undo fifty bead buttons along her spine. It wasn't a good way to keep distance between them.

"Let me help you."

She stiffened as he touched the first button at the back of her gown. It lay just where her bra strap would be, if she were wearing one. The gown left her shoulders bare, and swept to the floor in a glorious sea of twinkling sequins and shining satin, the skirt a little full but not bell-shaped, more suited to the old Hollywood-style of elegant evening wear. Crystal loved it.

Had loved it, she thought, as Mitch's fingers brushed the bare skin of her shoulders.

"These are tiny buttons," he murmured. "Why didn't they just put a zipper in here?"

"Uncle Martin says the beading is better craftsmanship done by hand, without the zipper to lie over. He says the effect is more smooth and dreamy," she replied, her heart racing.

"When I heard you'd opened up a bridal boutique, I thought Bess and Elle were probably the driving force behind you. I was very surprised to find out it was your uncle instead."

Crystal smiled. "Oh, Mom doesn't have the patience to sew, and brides would make her nervous. She's wonderful at hostessing parties, and socializing, but she'd be more suited to running a catering business. And Aunt Elle is a wonderful artist, but she needs absolute silence to create. There is nothing silent about an excited bride," she said with a laugh. "Uncle Martin learned a lot about sewing out of necessity. My grandparents were tailors in Germany, and during World War II they did less fine sewing and more repair work. Uncle Martin had two little sisters who needed clothes, but Grandma and Grandpa were busy making a living, so he figured he could sew up two pieces of material with a hole for a small head to poke through and two for arms." She noticed Mitch's fingers slowly moving down her dress as she spoke—the sensation gave her an agonizingly delicious thrill. "Uncle Martin admired the fashions coming out of France at the time, and decided if he could sew little girl dresses, it couldn't be much harder to do big girl dresses. He ended up with a nice business in inexpensive clothes that imitated French fashion."

"Does he still sew a lot?"

Crystal shook her head, realizing with a start that her entire back was now exposed. Mitch's fingers fought with a tiny button at her waist, and she reached to hold the front of her gown so the bodice wouldn't fall and leave her exposed. "He taught me how to sew when I was a child, and helped me with high school home ec projects. Occasionally, he'll help me with a difficult alteration on a bridal gown, and we do go over the catalogs together. He likes to go to market with me and pick out the next season's gowns. But Mom said once that when the family left Germany to get away from what was happening at the end of the war, he never sewed once he hit American soil."

"He didn't have to."

"I guess not. He worked his way through a small college, got a business degree, married the woman of his dreams, and when she died, he moved to Lover's Valley to live with us."

She stepped free of the gown, snatching up her robe to cover herself. Mitch laid the gown over a chair. "It was so pretty I hated to take it off of you."

Her eyelids lowered. "Thank you. You were very handsome yourself."

"You know, Crystal," he said huskily, moving to stand closer to her. "We're not like Uncle Martin. We're not doing this out of complete necessity."

"No. I suppose not."

"I mean," he said, putting his hands on her shoulders and pulling her closer to him, "I know we said there were many good reasons for us to get married, but it isn't like we were forced to do it."

"You have a point," she said, her body trembling as he tucked her head under his chin. She stared at the crisp white shirt that spread across his chest in a stiffly proud display of wedding finery. A black tie accented the formal attire. "We were pretty fancy for a gym, I guess."

He chuckled. "We would have been thirteen years ago, too. I had a great tux rented."

"I know. I picked it out."

"I wondered if you remembered."

"Oh, I did. In fact, I was torn with jealousy when I saw the picture of you and Kathryn in the Lover's Valley newspaper. You were a very handsome escort for a lovely prom queen."

His arms tightened around her. "Then I guess you know that this is the same style tux, right down to the tie."

"It seemed quite familiar." She snuggled up against him more tightly.

"You little minx," he said, laughing. "You knew very well I was trying to re-create the entire night we would have had together. I thought you hadn't noticed."

Putting her arms around his waist, she squeezed him gently, enjoying the feel of muscle and fit male. "It was perfect, Mitch. Thank you."

With one finger, he tipped her chin up and stared into her eyes. "So what do you think?"

"I think it was much better to be a bride than a prom date."

"Do you really?"

"Yes, I do," she assured him. "Even though I broke out in hives getting to the altar."

"And tossed your cookies for a week leading up to it. It was worth that?"

"The only thing I'll ever remember being tossed was my bouquet. How's that for a metaphor?"

"I love it," he said, sneaking his hands under her robe to feel her bare back. "I wouldn't have missed this for the world."

They melded against each other and he removed her robe. Crystal quickly undid his tie and stiff white shirt. She couldn't wait to unzip his trousers and pull off his shoes. He wanted to linger over the white garter belt, which flashed with delicate sequins holding up sheer white stockings, but she wouldn't let him. "I've waited for thirteen years for this," she said breathlessly, pulling him up onto the bed with her.

"Me, too," he answered, his lips against hers and his fingers in her hair.

They kissed fast, and hot, and hard. Crystal moaned, wanting Mitch more than ever. She urged him inside her. Gasping, they both stopped for a moment, staring into each other's eyes.

"Oh, my gosh," she said on a surprised whisper.

"The strangest feeling just passed over me that...we're truly one now. Really one being. Does that sound crazy?"

His smile said he felt the same way. "I was thinking along similar lines," he told her, swooping down for an instant to kiss her lips, and then each of her breasts. "I feel married. I feel...whole."

Joyful tears sprang into Crystal's eyes. "It's not what I thought it would be," she admitted. "It's so much better this way."

She began moving against him, encouraging him to stroke faster, go deeper. Together they found a rhythm they hadn't known before, a union of perfect harmony. "Oh, Mitch," she cried, never wanting it to end, because the moment was perfect, translucently alive with the explosion of happiness bursting inside her. Before she could admit that she wanted the climax, it swept over her, claiming her with abundant freedom to relax in her lover's arms and succumb to the passion.

"Crystal," he said on a tight groan, his body stiff as he buried himself deep inside her. "Crystal!" He went into her arms, surrendering to pleasure that seemed to shoot from every pore of his body. She was beneath him, accepting him, her passion fully encompassing him, and he thought he was going to lose his mind. His climax followed hers, and a yell tore loose inside him. Every muscle in his arms and legs seemed to go limp with the surge of completion that claimed him, but he made certain he didn't collapse on top of her.

Yet her arms reached to pull him to her, and he realized she didn't mind his weight against her. He accepted her offering and let himself totally relax. Pressing a gentle kiss against her temple, he felt her fingertips lightly stroking his back as if to calm him. He felt calm. In fact, he felt mended, somehow. No more Jekyll and Hyde.

I never expected to feel anything like this. This, this moment, is magic.

Chapter Seventeen

On Sunday morning, Mitch wanted to stay in bed forever with his new bride. "I don't mind getting up to feed the dogs and cats," he said. "I just want to find you still here when I get back. Right there, between the sheets."

She was nude underneath the sheet, so she let it fall to her waist as she sat up and rearranged the pillow behind her. "Are you certain you wouldn't rather do something else today?" she asked, making her tone sultry and teasing.

He pointed a finger at her. "Don't move. You look like a Renoir or one of those nude paintings painted by a great master. I want to find you just like that when I get back."

"Are you going to paint me?"

"I'm going to do better than that." He dashed out the back door. Mitch raced through the chore, sounding frantic as he filled the dog and cat bowls with dry food. He hurried inside to wash his hands, and Crystal laughed as he ran past the bed.

She fluffed her hair around her shoulders when

he paused to simply stare at her, drinking her in. "I could at least brush my teeth since you were so kind to offer to feed the pack."

"You're beautiful. I'm no artist, but if I were, I'd be whipping out the paints and canvas right now."

She rewarded his romantic talk with a smile. They'd drunk champagne and loved each other until the light hours of the morning. It had been a wonderful wedding night. Mitch crawled back in the bed beside his lovely bride.

"Maybe you're not the kind of artist that paints, but you do other amazing things with your hands," she murmured, allowing him to stroke her body the way he knew she liked. "Lover, surgeon—"

The phone rang, making both of them jump.

"Don't answer it," he said.

"I have to," she said on a laugh. "Although you give me great reason not to."

"It's my sisters. We can call them back."

"It's my mother. She's discovered we're not legally married and wants us to repeat the performance just to make doubly certain her only daughter is no longer an old maid," Crystal guessed.

"Don't answer it," he said. "We can tell her later that the wedding night was fully consummated and that you are married in the fullest sense of the word. Not that I remember being in bed with an old maid last night—"

"You're sweet, but we have to."

She reached over him to answer the phone, and

he took advantage of her position to stroke her breasts. With half an ear he listened to her say hello and then frowned as she swiftly sat up.

"Just a moment, please," he heard her say, her tone formal.

Handing him the phone, she said, "This is a call you kind of have to take, Mitch. It's your lawyer."

He took the phone from her, watching regretfully as she slid from the bed, her face suddenly sad. Covering the mouthpiece with his hand, he said, "Don't go far."

She smiled, but it wasn't the same happily-ever-after smile she'd worn since the wedding.

"As soon as I get back," Mitch said, "I'll help you with the packing for the cruise."

Crystal nodded. "All right. Kathryn's going to come over every day and feed the pet menagerie," she said, staring at a to-do list. She crossed something off. "I didn't trust Uncle Martin to do it. He overfeeds the pets by about a cup a day. But I don't think Kathryn was herself at the wedding. With the new baby, maybe I'm asking too much. Barney said he'd help her, but..." She turned to face him. "What do you think?"

"That you worry too much. If you haven't noticed, Barney is practically living with Kathryn and that infant. In fact, I think he morphed into that child's real father while we weren't looking. I hear wedding bells in the not-too-distant future, like quite possibly when we return from our honeymoon.''

She gasped, putting down the pad and pencil. "You know something you're not telling!"

"Never! I tell my wife everything," he said, looking extremely smug.

"You don't tell me everything. You're holding something back." Crystal lowered her gaze, appalled by what she'd said. "I didn't mean that the way it sounded."

He tried to take her in his arms, but she wasn't ready for that much closeness just yet.

"It's not that I'm keeping anything from you. I just haven't wanted to talk about tomorrow. And this last-minute call to meet with the family who is suing me isn't pleasant, Crystal. I'm going, but I'd give anything not to leave you. I want to stay here and pack for our honeymoon. I want to stay here and make love with you. Can you blame me for not wanting to talk about it? I'm a guy. I'd rather have sex than talk any old day.''

She knew he was avoiding the subject, but she couldn't help smiling at him. "Me, too. It's not just a guy thing.''

He sneaked a kiss. "I always wondered about that.''

"Wonder no longer." She wound her arms around him. "As a matter of fact—''

The phone rang again, and they stared at each other.

"Now I'm glad we booked a cruise," he told her.

"It will be a heck of a lot harder for anyone to call us while we're in the middle of the ocean."

She grinned. "That was not the original reason you suggested we take a cruise. You answer the phone this time. It's half yours now, anyway."

"Splitting phone duty. Did I agree to that?"

"I think it's redundant," she said as he picked up the phone. "As a doctor, aren't you always 'on call'?"

"Oh, ha ha. Hello?"

She watched his eyebrows rise, and momentarily contemplated how handsome he was. It was going to be sheer bliss to spend a week with him watching him wear little more than swim trunks. Lying on a beach in some romantic place with Mitch would be the closest thing to heaven on earth for her, she decided.

"Sure. Come on over. We're not doing anything except packing, and I have to leave in a little while, so now's the best time. Okay. Bye." He hung up the phone and grinned. "That was Bess. Your family wants to come over and give us our bon voyage gifts."

"Bon voyage gifts?" Crystal shook her head. "Are you sure you knew what you were getting into when you said 'I do'? I have the only family who would call at noon the day after our wedding to say they're bearing bon voyage gifts."

"As I recall, you accepted some risk as well. I'd call this whole thing even."

He tossed some T-shirts on the bed beside his

swim trunks and looked at her. "Anyway, if not for your family, we wouldn't be wearing gold rings, most likely. I was feeling pretty sorry for myself at the time. Since your mother began interfering in my life, I've had a lot more to feel good about."

"Perish the thought!" But Crystal laughed and laid sunglasses next to the suitcase.

"No, it's true. Before your aunt reintroduced us, I was depressed about the lawsuit, my baby sister was marrying a dope, and my other sister was engaged but in my heart I knew she wasn't happy. I think I thought that all Janet needed was a man to appreciate her, and then she'd be content. I noticed the sudden weight gain, but I...ignored it. I didn't want to think that she wasn't happy." They met each other's eyes for a shared moment of empathy. "The fact that my life has been totally turned around for the better since I met you again does not escape me. Notice I'm not all that worried about tomorrow, for example. Apprehensive, yes, but not worried. I'd rather not leave you today to go meet with my lawyer and the plaintiff's lawyer, but I know I have you to come home to, and that's why I know everything's going to be just fine, whichever way it goes."

"That's so sweet," she murmured. "You were supposed to be rescuing me from a life of utter spinsterhood."

"Well, it's nice to do my civic duty," he told her. "One less spinster roaming the streets, disturbing the population balance."

"Oh, hush!" She tossed a couple of beach towels at him. "Find a place in our suitcase for those."

He caught the towels. "Our suitcase. Our suitcase. I really, really like the sound of that."

Crystal hid a smile. "If it's our suitcase, then it's also our lawsuit."

He raised his head slowly, the smile gone as he laid the towels beside the suitcase. "Crystal," he said huskily. "I appreciate what you're trying to do. But it's my burden. I told you in the beginning that this in no way would affect you. I made certain with my lawyer that there was no way your assets could be affected. And that's as much as I want to talk about it."

"It's not about assets, Mitch. It's about what is ours. I shared the burden of my mother's cardiac problems. You helped me with that immeasurably."

"No, I didn't," he broke in. "She wanted me to do the surgery, and I couldn't. Wouldn't."

"So you think you don't deserve me being there for you right now?" Crystal shook her head. "That isn't logical. Nor is it the way I feel. People who keep things from each other don't stay together—" She broke off the second she realized what she'd said. The doorbell rang, and they stared at each other.

"That's your family bearing gifts," he said softly.

"Streamers and champagne to celebrate," she replied hesitantly.

"We have a lot to celebrate. Come on."

They went to the front door together, but Crystal suddenly felt that maybe it had all been just a wonderful dream. Any minute she would wake up.

Actually, she had. Because in that moment, she realized they'd all been playing their parts.

She'd been the only one who'd strayed from the script. They'd gotten married for many reasons, but none of them was love.

"Congratulations!" Bess cried as Mitch opened the door.

"Congratulations! Bon voyage!" Martin and Elle said merrily.

They each held a wrapped package, and their faces held nothing but happiness.

Okay, Crystal thought. *I can play my part. For their sakes.*

"NOW THAT THEY'RE GONE, I think we should open the gifts," Mitch said. Somehow the three tiny packages lying inside the suitcase made him nervous. "I know they said not to, but won't Customs want to know what's inside them?"

"I'm sure they've got X-ray machines."

He frowned at her calm tone of voice. "I was expecting a bottle of champagne. Something typical."

"From my family?" She laid a demure swimsuit over the gifts so they'd be hidden from Mitch.

"That one gift is smaller than my finger," Mitch noted. "It makes me the most nervous of all."

"I heard the best things come in small packages," she teased.

"Okay, what about that squishy one? It's at least the size of my palm."

"A sexy nightie, knowing my mother. Rest easy, Mitch."

"Okay, I wouldn't mind a sexy nightie."

"It's probably not for you, you know."

He squinted at her. "The one Uncle Martin gave us we definitely should open now. Roundish, odd-shaped, small—I don't know."

She pushed him gently away from the suitcase. "It's time for you to go, Mitch. You don't have time to open gifts. Besides which, I think you're avoiding leaving."

"Maybe I am." He sighed heavily. "I am."

"I know. I understand."

He thought about how much he'd rather stay here with her than leave. "Once we're on that boat, it's just me and you, babe. Me and you. The honeymoon starts tomorrow afternoon after the hearing."

She gazed at him, her eyes glowing. "It's okay, Mitch. I know. Go do what you have to do."

He nodded. There was nothing else to say.

"Flash your wedding ring," she said softly. "I want the respectability factor to kick in as much as possible."

"It doesn't work as well, considering I let their daughter die."

"Oh, God, Mitch." Her eyes went round. "You hid your pain well."

"I hid from the pain by staying busy planning for the wedding. I realized that just now. The cruise, my sisters, you and your family, I've hidden behind all this to keep from giving into the fear. But I can't hide anymore."

He felt his hands begin to shake, and knew that these were not the hands that had once skillfully held a surgeon's precision tools. The wedding band he wore was no armor against the fear that suddenly encircled his heart.

CRYSTAL FINISHED PACKING with a heavy heart. She closed the suitcase, her ears straining for the sound of Mitch's car in the drive. He had been so quiet when he left that she was worried. The old Mitch, the one who laughed and teased and had a Robin Williams bedside manner, had been reduced to a shadow.

He was facing a lot, and he was facing it alone. He would not allow her to help him. The best thing she could do was not be hurt by his withdrawal. Six weeks of emotional support, that's what she could give him. They had married for convenience and it had been a good thing for both of them.

The front door opened and he walked in. "Mitch!"

His face was gray, his eyes dark.

"Oh, my gosh!" she cried. "What happened?"

He shook his head. "It was very hard to face her parents. If you don't mind, I'm going to take a nap."

Before she could say anything, he went into their room and closed the door.

Her heart shattered.

It would take a great surgeon to put her heart back together—and unfortunately, he had just shut her out.

CONCERN KEPT CRYSTAL from waking Mitch that night. Instead, she crawled into bed next to him as quietly as she could. Normally, he reached for her and held her in his arms, even when he slept, but now was different. He didn't reach for her, and she didn't reach out to him.

The next morning, he left while she was still asleep. She looked for a note, but there was nothing. The dogs and cats had been fed, their water changed to fresh.

The tickets for the cruise lay on the kitchen counter. Crystal hung on to the thought that after today's hearing, she and Mitch would be on a boat in the middle of the ocean. Just the two of them.

And then maybe they could begin the start of their marriage. Because in the night a new hope had grown in Crystal's heart. They'd married to shield themselves from certain unhappy factors in their lives, but after today, those factors would no longer exist. Maybe, just maybe, while they were in the middle of nothing but blue sea, the romance could blossom between them again.

She desperately hoped so, because if it did, she wanted to tell Mitch the truth. She didn't want a divorce. She wanted to start their marriage on their honeymoon. As if she were turning back a clock so that the hours before didn't matter as much, she hoped their real marriage could start not in the gym, where so much of the past had been, but on their honeymoon, where so much of the future could be.

CRYSTAL SAT BY THE FRONT door, waiting for Mitch to return. She had the suitcase in the car, the tickets in hand. A list for Kathryn lay in the kitchen, detailing the pets' feeding schedule.

"Suntan lotion," she murmured. "I forgot to pack suntan lotion." It was getting late. They needed to leave for the airport. She got up and occupied her racing mind by selecting a bottle of lotion from the bathroom cabinet and taking it out to the car.

After she packed it into the suitcase, she went back inside to pace some more. She wished she knew how Mitch's meeting was going!

A red flashing light on the answering machine caught her eye. She'd missed a phone call while she was outside. Punching the button, her breath held when she realized the call was from Mitch.

"Good news! We didn't actually have a hearing. The plaintiffs decided they didn't want to pursue a suit or claim against me. Apparently, they changed their minds after our meeting yesterday. It had something to do with the fact that I'd just gotten married. They said that they'd realized that suing me wasn't going to bring their daughter back, that they knew I had done my best to help her. In the end, they said they knew how much I'd cared for her, and that they hadn't meant to take their pain out on me. I'm free, Crystal! I'm free! Anyway, you go on to the airport—I've got some last-minute paperwork I have to finish and I'll meet you there.''

The message clicked off. Crystal smiled, grabbed her purse and the tickets, kissed the dogs and cats goodbye, and hurried out the door.

The past was about to be laid to rest forever.

AT THE AIRPORT, Crystal glanced at the clock. Mitch should have arrived by now. The boarding calls had become more urgent, as the plane door was within moments of being closed. She'd already checked in the suitcase.

''Ma'am, you need to board,'' said the woman who was holding the gate door open. ''It's now or never.''

''Oh, my gosh,'' Crystal said. ''My husband isn't here!''

''I'm sorry. I have to close the door.''

What should she do? Obviously, Mitch had gotten held up in traffic or something. She'd tried calling his cell phone, but he hadn't answered.

''He can meet you later. That way you won't lose both your airplane tickets,'' the woman suggested.

''I guess…you're right.'' Crystal glanced behind her. Mitch wasn't running urgently toward the gate. She didn't know what to do. She glanced again, knowing the woman couldn't wait another moment to shut the gate.

As if it were only yesterday, Crystal remembered that she'd waited on Mitch once before. She'd kept straining to see him, but he'd never come. And the prom had never happened for her. It had all been over.

But this was different. There was an explanation…there had to be…

"Ma'am," the woman said insistently.

"Okay." Crystal stepped forward and handed over her ticket. "I can cruise by myself if I have to." She'd call again before boarding the cruise ship.

"I'm sure that won't be necessary," the woman said with a smile. "Your groom wouldn't dream of not showing up for you."

Chapter Eighteen

Quayside in Florida, Crystal boarded the cruise liner. It was a beauty, big and colorfully decorated. People said goodbye to loved ones, laughing and happy to be going on a spectacular voyage.

Coldness seeped into Crystal as she went to her cabin. It was her cabin now. There had been no message for her from Mitch, though she hadn't really expected there to be. His mother had sounded worried when Crystal called, but as far as she knew, Mitch was fine. She had no explanation for him not showing up.

But Crystal knew why Mitch wasn't coming. Their marriage of convenience had been two-sided, and both sides had been fulfilled. Her mother had made a wonderful recovery, and the suit against Mitch had been put aside. He'd said a wife would give him a sense of respectability and solidness, but worries like that were now behind him.

There was no reason for them to continue their marriage. She might have realized she was in love with him and wanted their marriage to last, but it took two people to want that goal.

She went into her cabin and closed the door to wait for the ship to sail.

THE NURSE SPONGED SWEAT from Mitch's brow. The skin above his left eyelid twitched as he stared down at a sleeping Kathryn. He had no choice but to force himself past the fear. Kathryn's life depended on it.

He should have turned his pager off when he'd left the courthouse. He should never have returned the call when he'd seen it was the hospital number on the pager. He'd be on a ship now in the middle of the ocean with his bride—but no. Mitch had tried to call Crystal, but she'd already left. He'd left a message with her uncle, in hopes she'd call home when he didn't show up.

Kathryn had wanted him to perform the emergency surgery on her heart. Violent pain in her chest had sent her to her doctor. When she'd learned that she had a defective aortic valve, a weakness that needed repair, she had insisted she wanted no other doctor than Mitch. Ron Halberstam hadn't taken offense, remembering that there was history between the two of them. He'd tracked Mitch's pager number to get him the message.

Ron was here with Mitch, as he'd said he would be. Mitch was comforted by that, but the painful fact of operating again loomed large in front of him. Why Kathryn? Why a woman he cared so much about? He hadn't even had time to breathe a deep sigh of relief from the court case...and he could only hope that Martin had been able to get hold of Crystal to let her know what had happened.

Otherwise, the past would still be with them... most likely forever.

He said a quick prayer, and picked up the laser.

SEVERAL HOURS LATER, Mitch checked in on his patient. "How are you feeling?"

"Like I had heart surgery," she replied, her voice raspy from the recently removed respirator. She managed a weak smile for him. "Mitch, thank you."

"No problem. I was happy to do it."

He neared the bed, and she looked up at him. "It was a problem. You should be on your honeymoon."

"I'm going on my honeymoon." He sat next to her bed and took her hand. "Crystal wouldn't have wanted me to leave without making sure you were fine."

"It seems like I'm always keeping you two apart," she said sadly. "I know I was being selfish, but Mitch, there's nobody else I could trust to operate on me. I was so scared—"

"It's fine. I'm glad you caught me before I left. The truth is, Kathryn, I believe that this time, you've brought Crystal and I closer together. I'm pretty sure that's how it's all going to pan out."

"You're here, and she's on your honeymoon. I don't think you're closer together, Mitch."

"Maybe not at this moment, but I wasn't fully in the marriage yet, and I don't know that I could have been. I've been hiding behind my wedding plans to keep from thinking about the fact that I wasn't doing what I was born to do, which is to be a doctor. The crazy thing is, when you're a doctor, sometimes you have to be healed, too. And I hadn't healed. You forced me to become a doctor again, Kathryn. I might have ignored my skill forever if it hadn't been for you."

"You're being very kind, I think."

"No, I'm not. When I got the message that you required surgery and wanted only me to perform it, in spite of knowing about the lawsuit, I had to reward your faith. And more important, Crystal's. She never stopped believing in me. In the end, I was healed." He laughed, every word he spoke giving him a renewed sense of rightness. "It feels great, Kathryn. You can't know how great it feels to know that I can now be the husband Crystal deserves."

"You'd best go catch that boat, then."

He smiled at her. "Barney's wearing out the carpet in the waiting room. Can I send him in? You're not really supposed to have visitors when you're in this section, but I could sneak him in for two minutes, if you'd like that."

"I'd very much like that." The most delighted smile he'd seen Kathryn wear in a long time transformed her face. "I love him, Mitch."

"I know you do. It's obvious to everyone."

"I don't know that he'll want to be with me forever. I know he always wanted to be a bachelor. But he's so good to my baby, and he treats me like a queen. I've never been this happy."

Mitch's smile broadened. "From prom queen to Barney's queen. He looked pretty happy to me to give up his bachelor's membership card to be the king for a queen and her little princess."

Happiness glowed in her eyes. "Do you really think so?"

"Yeah. I know so. I have no doubts at all that while I'm on my honeymoon, you're going to be pampered the way I'd want my patient to be."

"Tell Crystal that I'm sorry, so sorry," Kathryn said, her joy dimming a bit. "And that Barney's going to go over every day and feed her pet menagerie, and that—"

"Kathryn. If you start worrying about little things that aren't important, I'm not going to let Barney come in."

"Psst!" sounded from the doorway.

"Barney!" Kathryn cried with delight.

"I snuck in, Doc," the hulking football player said. "I had to see her."

Mitch grinned at Kathryn. "Crystal and I will drop you a postcard. Enjoy your new life."

"I will. You do the same."

"Two minutes," he told Barney on the way out.

"Thanks, Doc," Barney said, his eyes on Kathryn.

Mitch grinned and hurried out. With any luck, he'd be in Crystal's arms tonight.

He hoped that he'd been right when he'd told Kathryn that Crystal would have wanted him to stay behind. It was a very awkward start to a marriage he wanted more than anything.

THE LAYOVER IN KEY WEST would only last the day, so Crystal decided to put on shorts and take a look around a place that was renowned for being a good walking town. Opening her suitcase, she saw the gifts to her and Mitch from Bess, Elle and Martin. Tears jumped into her eyes. They were gag gifts, she knew, but all the same, it hurt that her family had believed that she and Mitch were going to be together forever. Even though that was the original agreement between them, a rosy glow of happiness had overtaken her, making her want to believe that she and Mitch would stay together.

Pushing the three packages aside, she vowed not to think about it as much as possible. Of course, it wasn't easy to ignore the realization that she was, again, Lover's Valley's most conspicuous spinster.

She'd go back to dressing brides for their happily-ever-afters.

At night, she'd go home to her five cats, three dogs, lovebirds and the painted teacup she drank out of when she sat in her living room at night thinking about her business.

She'd be happy.

No. She'd be heartbroken.

SHE WAS BENT OVER brushing out her hair when a knock on the cabin door shocked her out of her sad thoughts. "I didn't order anything," she murmured. "Who is it?"

"Special delivery," a muffled voice called.

Hope leapt in her breast. Maybe it was a message from Mitch. A telegram? She pulled open the door. "Mitch!" she screamed, jumping into his arms.

"Ah. That was the longest flight of my life," he said, burying his face in her hair. "I was afraid you wouldn't open the door."

"Where were you?" Crystal asked, pulling back to look into his face.

"Did you get a message from Uncle Martin?"

She shook her head, but her heart was thrilling inside. "No."

"Kathryn had to have emergency surgery for an aortic abnormality."

"Oh, no!" Crystal slid out of his arms to stand in front of him. "I could tell she wasn't herself at our wedding."

"She wanted me to perform the surgery."

"Oh." Crystal caught her breath. "And so she's now in better shape than she was before."

The frown he'd worn upon hearing she hadn't received his message smoothed away. "You have so much faith in me."

"Well done, Dr. McStern. I'm proud of you." Joy blossomed inside her.

"You're not upset that you had to start your honeymoon without your groom?"

She shook her head. "I'd expect nothing less from you. Poor Kathryn."

"She was very upset that twice now she's come between us."

"I hope you alleviated her fears." Winding her arms around her groom, she said, "It's my prognosis that there's nothing for any of us to be afraid of anymore."

He kissed the tip of her nose. "I'd say that's a correct long-term diagnosis, Mrs. McStern."

"I love you, Mitch," she softly said, her heart singing with shining joy.

"I love you, Crystal. I always have, and I always will."

He kissed her, and she knew she'd never been so happy. "Let the honeymoon begin," she told him. "We have some good luck gifts from my family to open."

"I'll send for some champagne while we open."

She pulled out the packages with a smile. "They won't be the usual gifts, I'm sure."

"I'd be very disappointed if your family became typical."

She handed him the gift from Elle first. "It's the smallest so we'll start here."

"After she blew you away with your own china pattern, I'm glad she scaled back." Tossing the paper onto the bed, he held up a small piece of satin. "This looks suspiciously like something designed for you. It's too small to blow your nose on, and too big to wear to bed with me."

"It's a thong." Crystal snatched it out of his hand as he held it aloft. "I can only hazard a guess that Aunt Elle believes she is contributing to my trousseau."

"I love Aunt Elle. She's got the right idea." He raised his eyebrows and looked at the thong. "Model it for me."

"Maybe later." Crystal wasn't ready to commit to that with her new groom just yet.

"Promise?"

"Okay," she said with a laugh. "And I hope in this package there's something for you to wear."

The tag read From Bess. She unwrapped it, holding up black swim trunks. "I don't think this will fit you," she said. "And yet, I think that's my mother's intention."

He held it to his waist. "Do you get the impression that your family wants us wearing as little as possible on our honeymoon?"

Crystal smiled. "All I can tell you is that my family is a little wacky, and I hope you will never regret marrying the girl across the street."

"I could never regret it. Let's see what Uncle Martin deemed appropriate for honeymooning." He unwrapped the final gift and held up a set of plastic handcuffs.

He and Crystal stared at each other before bursting into laughter.

"I don't think we need these after all," Mitch said, dropping the handcuffs to the floor and taking Crystal into his arms.

"I don't think so, either," Crystal breathlessly agreed.

They melted into a kiss that led to a wonderfully romantic afternoon in bed—champagne, handcuffs and thong, notwithstanding.

"I forgot to tell you that Janet is engaged to Ron Halberstam," Mitch murmured against Crystal's ear hours later.

"I'm so glad for her!"

"And I want you to know," Mitch continued, "that I'm sending her back to your store to get her gown."

"You're not afraid I'll jinx this engagement?" Crystal asked with a smile.

"Oh, no," he said, and Crystal's blood fired at the look in her husband's eyes. "This time, everything is going to be just fine."

And this time, Crystal knew it would be, too.

Presenting...

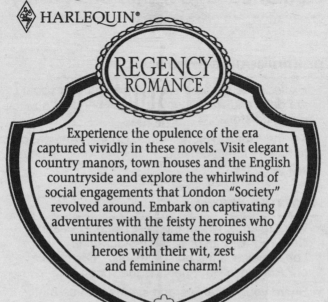

REGENCY ROMANCE

Experience the opulence of the era captured vividly in these novels. Visit elegant country manors, town houses and the English countryside and explore the whirlwind of social engagements that London "Society" revolved around. Embark on captivating adventures with the feisty heroines who unintentionally tame the roguish heroes with their wit, zest and feminine charm!

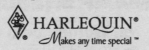

HARLEQUIN®

AMERICAN ◆ ROMANCE®

and **Muriel Jensen**

present

WHO'S THE
DADDY?

𝒜t a festive costume ball, three identical
sisters meet three masked bachelors.

ℰach couple has a taste of true love behind
the anonymity of their costumes—but
only one will become parents
in nine months!

Find out who it will be!

November 2000
FATHER FEVER #858

January 2001
FATHER FORMULA #855

March 2001
FATHER FOUND #866

HARLEQUIN®
Makes any time special ™

COMING NEXT MONTH

#849 SECRET BABY SPENCER by Jule McBride
Return to Tyler
Businessman Seth Spencer was surprised to see Jenna Robinson in Tyler,
Wisconsin, especially once he discovered she was pregnant—with his
baby! Though she claimed she planned to marry another, Seth was not
about to let Jenna's secret baby carry any other name but Spencer.

#850 FATHER FEVER by Muriel Jensen
Who's the Daddy?
Was he the father of Athena Ames's baby? Was the enigmatic beauty even
really expecting? Carefree bachelor David Hartford was determined to
uncover the truth and see if Athena was behind his sudden case of father
fever!

#851 CATCHING HIS EYE by Jo Leigh
The Girlfriends' Guide to...
Plain Jane Emily Proctor knew her chance had come to catch the eye of
her lifelong crush. With a little help from friends—and one great big
makeover—could Emily finally win her heart's desire?

#852 THE MARRIAGE PORTRAIT by Pamela Bauer
Happily Wedded After
When Cassandra Carrigan accepted Michael McFerrin's marriage of
convenience proposal, she'd thought it was a sound business deal. But
spending night after night with her "husband" soon had her hoping
Michael would consider mixing a little business with a lot of pleasure....

Visit us at www.eHarlequin.com